Praise for *Clay*

Clay will seize your heart and your imagination while becoming your friend. *Clay* will awaken you to the amazing truth that there is something really special about you. *Clay* will convince you that becoming yourself is what living is all about.

Fil Anderson, author of *Running on Empty*

Clay powerfully captures a person's journey (particularly a teenager's pursuit) toward purpose and identity. It is real and engaging. I recommend it.

Ty Saltzgiver, Senior Vice President of Young Life

Ned uses the art of metaphor to mine the depths of our common experience. In the personification of Clay we find the fear, loneliness, hope, and longing of our fundamental pursuit of meaning and identity in life – this little story will linger in your soul long after you turn its last page because it is true, and true things stick.

Rick Lawrence, Executive Editor of GROUP Magazine, author of *Sifted* and *Shrewd*

I found the work to be wonderfully creative. Several times, I pulled aside to read portions to my family and comment to them how much I was enjoying *Clay*. The story kept me guessing, wondering how it would end. When I turned the final page and read the last line, I "sliced" a smile and closed the book, contented.

Marty Machowski, author of
Long Story Short and *The Gospel Story Bible.*

For anyone feeling ordinary, here's a story that will redefine you. For anyone searching for purpose, here's a story that will redirect you. For anyone longing for more life, here's a story that will renew you. It's not the lyrical beauty of Erickson's prose or even the "page-turner" storyline that gripped my heart – it was the gradual realization that I am Clay. We are all clay.

Alan D. Wright, author of *Free Yourself,*
Be Yourself and *Lover of My Soul*

Clay is a book that you will happily add to the list of classic reads that you enjoy returning to again and again. Ned has a truly sweet and pure way of raising our curiosity, drawing us in to Clay's beauty and its winding path below the surface of things. It is the story of our calling, design and purpose. This book most definitely will awaken the sleeping child in many a reader. It did for me!

Michael R. Jordan, Pastor of Worship
and Creative Arts, Greenwood Community
Church, Greenwood Village, CO

This book is simply a gift. Clay's story is unique and familiar, gut-wrenching and buoyant. With its vibrant language, compelling narrative, and provocative questions of meaning and purpose, we find upon turning the final page that we, like Clay, have been transformed.

Dr. Joan F. Mitchell, Master Teacher and co-author of *Bridging English*

Clay is reminiscent of C.S. Lewis' Narnia – decorated with wonder, but founded on unshakeable truth. As Clay embarks on his search for purpose, every reader will see bits of themselves in his adventure. If you've ever questioned your purpose in life, doubted your value to the world, or simply longed for something more, then Clay's journey towards "being made" will delight you, teach you, and inspire you.

Greg Lisson, Director of Christian Life at the Wesleyan School, Norcross, GA

Clay
Copyright © 2013 by Ned Erickson

Illustrations by Elizabeth Northcut Williams
Front and back cover design by Robert Milam
Cover Photo by Trevor Mork
Back Cover Photo by Elizabeth Northcut Williams
Author photo by Elizabeth Northcut Williams
Interior layout and e-book by Lisa Parnell

ISBN: 978-0-9911792-0-6 (paperback)

ISBN: 978-0-9911792-1-3 (e-book)

For information contact
LANDover Books
851 W. 5th Street
Winston-Salem, NC 27101

Printed in the United States of America
Printed by CreateSpace, an Amazon.com Company
Available from Amazon.com, CreateSpace.com,
and other retail outlets

20 19 18 17 16 15 14 13   1 2 3 4 5

Ned Erickson

LANDover Books

In memory of
BERNARD SARCHET

~

Dedicated to
ANNA ROSE AND DAVID

Contents

Prologue

Sitting by the Fire

WE WERE SITTING by the fire in the room he called the den. I remember it vividly: the embers beating like a heart, their sleepy *hiss*, the orange glow dimming in Grandpa's cloudy eyes as he finished his incredible story, the one I'm about to tell you.

He believed every word. "When you experience something of that magnitude you find yourself capable of many things," he explained. Perhaps that's why I didn't believe it right away. Nothing like that has ever happened to me. Not that my experience changes things. It's just, at some point you may begin to wonder if this is all made up. I did. When I heard it, I wondered. Even with the proof right here before me, I still find it hard to believe.

But now that I've finally sat down to write, I realize how foolish it's been to let my doubts get in the way. After all, though the outcome affects me, the story isn't mine.

It's not even Grandpa's for that matter. It's Clay's. He's the hero in Grandpa's tale. That's the unbelievable part. You see, before Clay was made, he was just that – a lump of clay. And I guess you could say he was *made* at the beginning. He was *made of clay*, which is really just another word for *mud*, which isn't really a nice thing to call anybody (even when it's accurate). What's important to note is that, to Grandpa, Clay was real. He could twist, jump, stretch, roll, walk, talk and whistle, just like you and me.

Now, I imagine that some of you are thinking: how can a piece of clay do that? That's impossible! Well, that's what I thought, too, until I came to realize that was the point Grandpa was trying to make. What happened is incredible.

Part One —
The Deposit

He'd watch the stars sparkle
from their spots in the universe...

The Whistle

MANY YEARS AGO, Grandpa's grandfather planted an orchard along the banks of Mule Lick Creek just up the road from Buena Vista. He had hopes for it. Apples mainly. We were growers back then; though really, it was the rain and the sun that did the growing part. My ancestors pruned and picked, which is involvement enough to constitute the title. To be fair, that was all you could expect from them. Since the beginning, no one on earth has grown an apple without water and light doing the work.

What apples weren't sold as apples were baked into pies or fixed into preserves or smushed into apple butter (their specialty) or pressed into cider or dried into chips. Have you heard of *Mrs. Farmer's Famous Apple Butter*? That's my family: the Farmers. I have a different last name because my Grandpa had three girls, but my first name is the same as his: Ned. I've always been proud of that fact.

Grandpa was seven years old the summer his life changed forever. Clay's too, but we'll get to that. What matters here is that Ned was at the age when freedom met possibility: old enough to explore his family's property without adult supervision, but young enough to believe that impossible just meant it hadn't yet been tried. Like many boys his age, Ned was governed by the most powerful elixir known to man, youthful curiosity.

By the time his family bumped up the road to the orchard house, Ned had nearly quivered out of his skin thinking about the adventures awaiting him in the forests, hills and streams. It was what put the crane in his neck when he strained for that first glimpse of what promised to be a summer he would never forget.

And perhaps it was the straining or just the expectation in the posture, but it was precisely in that position that Ned heard *the whistle*. Coming from the banks of Mule Lick Creek, the tune was unlike any bird he ever heard. Of course, Ned imagined a bird. He never imagined a sound like that could come from a thing like clay. He'd find out soon enough.

Clay would, too. Not about whistles but about boys. Whistling came as natural to Clay as blinking does to you and me. It was a daily activity. To Clay, whistling made the nice days nicer and the dreary ones tolerable, so there was never reason not to. Plus, he was good at it: his *tur-a-lee, chir, chir-a-lee* could make a bluebird blush; his *cheerily, cheerily, cherrio, chee* could drop the worm right out of a robin's beak; and his *wheet, whittle, wheet, wheet* could compete with any house finch on the block. Lately, he had been working on a whistle of his own design. It started with a low flutter, almost like a drum roll – *trrrrrllllllll* – before skyrocketing to a *wheet!* Clay liked the way the sounds fit together. The combination filled him with anticipation every time the air fluttered out the slice of his mouth, which happened to be why he whistled the tune the moment he saw a boy's neck crane his direction – Clay was anticipating.

There was something about the boy that made him wonder.

Clay had been wondering, in fact, for some time. It usually happened during the wee hours while he stared through the leaves at the great, wide sky above him. From his spot by Mule Lick Creek, he'd watch the stars sparkle from their spots in the universe. He'd shudder at their beauty. Though, sometimes their distance produced in him a longing that was almost too large to bear. A feeling of lonely that left him wondering if he was missing something, if there was more to life than just being Clay. And many nights he'd lie awake into the wee hours, wondering what that something could be.

The wonderings curled around his mind like a question mark. They'd linger like wet leaves that only fingers could peel away – curious fingers like the ones attached to the boy straining his neck out the bumping-along horse cart. That was the meaning of Clay's whistle: the wondering if the boy could make the lonely go away?

A Day Beyond Belief

UPON ARRIVING AT the wooden farm-house, Ned performed his chores with such speed and vigor that Father, with a grin, suggested giving the boy a few more. "What's got into him?" asked Mother, stacking dishes in the cupboard. Father just smiled because he knew. He, too, had been a boy once. As for Ned, he was out the door, down the hill and to the creek faster than it took to put the punctuation mark on this sentence.

The banks along Mule Lick Creek were overgrown with saplings, sticker bushes and stinging nettles. It created a kind of dual-purpose barrier that both sheltered it from the rest of the world and shielded the rest of the world from it. Passing through was like passing from one reality to another.

Clay lived in a shady spot along the bank in what's called a deposit. Over the years, the mountains above Mule Lick Creek eroded, bringing down tiny particles in the forms of sand, silt and clay. Most traveled downstream to a river that emptied into a bay that drained into an ocean. Other particles settled to the bottom of the creek and formed what's called a bed. Some collected along the bank to become a deposit. Clay didn't know this at the time, but the kind of deposit he came from was called Brownstone.

Clay did know, however, that he could twist, jump, stretch, roll, walk, talk and whistle. That was the remarkable thing about him: Clay could shape into most anything. Although at the moment when Ned splashed up the bank, Clay wasn't doing any of the things clay could do; he was simply resting in his deposit listening to the music the water made.

Clay loved the songs of the current. When the creek was high, it was like the clapping of ten thousand leaves. (Listen next time it's windy, and you'll hear the leaves clap. It sounds just like rushing water.) When the water was low, the creek sounded like bells. Sometimes the water sang quietly like a dream. Currently, Ned's splashes made it sound like cymbals.

Hearing the clatter, Clay rose in a mound and poked himself eyes. Ten feet downstream, a boy was rummaging through the bushes for a bird nest that didn't exist. Impulsively, Clay rolled a head, molded a torso, sprouted arms, launched legs, cupped ears, pinched a nose and sliced a mouth – thinking the boy might find it easier to relate to something boy-sized and human-like. Checking his reflection, Clay blinked at the light gleaming off his smooth head. *What was he missing?* He looked again at the boy. *Hair!* Clay hunted the riverbank for a remedy. A patch of fern caught his eye. Plucking two branches, he considered where to stick them when, suddenly, the boy twirled around.

"Oh my," said Ned, more surprised than afraid.

Startled, Clay flapped the leafy stems for balance while the rest of him went both ways at once then slipped to the mud in a great big plop.

Ned giggled. "Were you trying to fly?" he asked, watching Clay frantically put himself together – too frantically it turned out, because he left an ear in the mud and switched an arm for a leg. "You're clay," said Ned with amazement. "I'm a boy."

"I'm Clay," said Clay through the slice of his mouth.

Ned reached out his hand and shook Clay's leg. "Pleased to meet you."

"Oh! Excuse me," said Clay, quickly rearranging.

"Wow!" said Ned. "Can you twist into a snake?"

Clay twisted into a snake.

"Can you roll into a ball?"

Clay rolled.

Ned pointed to an oak tree. "Can you climb that?"

In reply, Clay transformed back into a snake and slinked up the trunk.

Delighted, Ned clambered after him.

"What do you think?" asked Clay after he changed back to boy-sized and human-like.

"You're better than I could imagine," Ned answered with a twinkle in his eye. He whispered an idea into Clay's slightly cockeyed ear.

Clay's slice of a mouth curled upwards. Then, stretching snake-like once again, he slithered along the branch over the creek, fastened his ends and drooped his middle like a *U* that had lost a fight with a taffy-pulling machine.

Grinning with approval, Ned slid down to Clay's middle. "Make sure you swing me high," he said, pumping his legs. Obliging, Clay rocked back and forth, then launched Ned through the air, over the shoals, and into the deep pool beyond them.

Ned burst to the surface and slapped the water, shouting: "Again!"

So they did.

That Evening

MOTHER RANG THE bell a third time.

"Come to supper," said Ned. They were side by side on a flat rock in the middle of the creek. "That's what you do with a new friend."

Clay wasn't sure. He had never eaten supper before, but he was too excited about the last part, the part about being a new friend, to let a small technicality like the fact that he didn't have a stomach get in the way. He wanted to be with Ned. And here was Ned's hand waiting for Clay's to join it. So without the certainty of knowing what he was getting into, Clay coiled into a spring and sprang over the water. Then changing back, he skipped with Ned up the hill to the orchard house.

Ned's sister, Betsy, was reading on the porch. She was ten though her parents said she acted at times like a sixteen year old. They didn't always mean it as a compliment. Her interests included things like nail polish and books. Ned's were more bullfrogs and sling-shots. But despite their differences, the two got along fairly well, which doesn't entirely explain why she ran inside screaming "disgusting" and calling out for Mother when Ned showed up with a boy-sized blob of mud.

"What on earth have you gotten yourself into?" Mother cried, barring the door with her short but sturdy frame.

"Nothing," said Ned.

"Nothing my left foot. You're filthy," she said before gasping. "And don't you dare think for one minute I'm going to let you bring that *thing* into my clean house."

"He's not a thing. He's Clay," said Ned, as if that would explain.

"I can see that. Get it off my porch," she said, pointing a scolding finger.

"He's my friend," said Ned.

"Young man, you always did have a wild imagination. But if you think I'm going to let a pile of dirt through my door, you have another thing coming."

Father wrung his strong calloused hands in a towel as he came up behind her.

"He's not a pile of dirt. He's real. Tell him," said Ned, nudging Clay.

But Clay couldn't do anything around people who didn't believe he could.

"He can speak," said Ned. "He's just a little shy."

"Sure he can," said Father, squatting to Ned-height, "but Mother's right. You go on inside and wash up."

Ned shrugged obediently then whispered to Clay, "I'll eat fast," before slipping between his parents' legs.

Mother gave Father a glance that said *I don't think this relationship should be encouraged.* Father looked back as if to say *It will pass.*

That evening once the dishes were washed and put away, Ned met Clay by the bridge over Mule Lick Creek then crossed to the other side where they spent the last remnants of daylight together. Ned had this idea in his head of catching fireflies. Clay had never heard of such a thing. He'd seen fireflies, of course, but the idea of catching them had never crossed his mind. Though once they started, Clay wondered why he hadn't thought of it before.

The way they went about it was like this: Clay would hand a miniature portion of himself to Ned, who would then hurl the little Clay into the air. Once airborne, Clay would speed toward the target and enclose around the bug in a sphere while on the ground the rest-of-Clay formed into a catcher's mitt. They caught several fireflies this way, Ned poking holes in Clay-the-ball so he and the rest-of-Clay could watch the insect light up the inside like a flashing sun before releasing the creature back to Nature.

"Why didn't you move in front of my parents?" asked Ned through a yawn.

"I think I only move to the people who believe I can move," answered Clay, letting the last of the fireflies free.

"You move to me," said Ned.

Clay's slice of mouth curved into a smile.

Stars began to sparkle from their spots in the universe.

Mother called to Ned from the other side of the creek.

"I guess it's time for bed," said Ned, frowning. He took a step toward the house before turning back around. "Clay?"

"Yes," said Clay.

"Can we do this day again tomorrow?"
"I'd like that," said Clay.
"Me, too," said Ned.

Crick and Craw

A HEAVY FEELING came over Clay as Ned disappeared down the hill and out of sight. It came from the realization that the boy had filled somehow the missing part in Clay. Unfortunately, now that the boy was gone, the empty space had gotten bigger with only loneliness to fill it. And the loneliness hurt, especially with the helplessness that accompanied it. The feeling filled every mineral and molecule of his being with an absence that came over and out of him in a long, sad whistle, which left him hollow inside.

Branches rustled in an apple tree.

Clay wasn't alone, after all.

"Crick, would you look at that?"

"Never seen anything like it, Craw," cackled Crick from his branch.

"Hey you, Mud Pie," crowed Craw, flapping a wing.

Clay faced the two crows above him. "I'm not a Mud Pie."

"Could have fooled me," crowed Craw.

"I'm Clay."

Crick gave Craw a chicken wing. "He says that as if it's something to be proud of."

"You know what's another word for Clay?" crowed Craw, dropping to a lower branch. "Mud."

"Stop it!" cried Clay.

"Just doing our part," crowed Crick, not so innocently.

"We were worried you forgot," cawed Craw.

"Forgot what?"

"Who you are," Crick crowed.

"Who am I?" asked Clay.

"Our point exactly," cawed Craw.

"What do you mean?" asked Clay.

"You and that boy," crowed Crick.

"He's my friend," said Clay, with less confidence than he would have liked to muster.

"He's a boy," crowed Crick.

"So."

"He won't stay one forever," cawed Crick. "Sooner or later you'll just be dirt to him."

"From dust you came, to dust you will return," crowed Craw, crossing his wing solemnly.

"What happens then?" asked Clay.

"Nothing," cawed Crick. His marble eyes flashed cold light.

The word chilled Clay to the bones he didn't have.

"Think of it this way: you won't be any different than what you are right now," cackled Crick.

"It's not true," stammered Clay.

"Of course it is. Take a look around."

Clay couldn't help it; he did. Lifeless dirt was all around.

"Don't let it weigh on you," Crick cawed. "Nothing lasts forever. We all got to face it."

"Don't remind me," crowed Craw.

"Exactly. Never let the inevitable get you down." Crick lifted off the branch. As if to demonstrate, he glided across the creek, rose on a wind gust then swooped back down.

"So what's the point?" asked Clay.

Craw and Crick's onyx eyes gave each other a look. "There is no point," they rasped.

A chill went through Clay. "So why am I here?" he asked meekly.

"Now that's a good question," crowed Crick.

"What's the answer?"

"That's for you to find out," Craw crowed.

Crick ruffled his feathers. "Let's get out of here, Craw. All this talk about nothing depresses me."

"Wait!" Clay called after them.

"Enjoy it while it lasts," crowed Craw, lifting into the air.

"Come back!" Clay waved. But he might as well have been waving good-bye. The two black crows had become pinholes in the night sky.

Summer Doesn't Last Forever

CLAY SLUMPED TO his deposit. The fullness of the day had left him too tired to sleep, which doesn't seem possible unless it's happened to you. That night it happened to Clay. Never had his deposit felt so uncomfortable. It was lumpy with fears and worries and questions without answers. The *why am I here's* and *would Ned come backs* and *what's the point of it all anyways* were like uninvited guests who refused to leave. And no matter how hard Clay tried to ignore them, they kept poking him in the back.

However, the next morning when Ned arrived and leapt into the two arms Clay had hardly enough time to sprout, it was like all his uncomfortable worries had been imagined, and there was nothing in the future to fear.

Ned and Clay's second day continued into what became a whole string of glorious days. That summer, the two were inseparable. Blazing trails, building forts, and creating games out of thin air: they explored worlds both real and imagined with only daylight to stop them. And though one was clay and the other was human, the two held much in common. Both were still forming, still capable of becoming most anything, and the end seemed so far off – even on the day it almost happened.

Creek hopping Ned called it. One afternoon along a shallower section upstream, they leapt rock to rock, counting as they went. It was a challenge, more so for Ned. Clay was so nimble he had little fear of falling – though doing so would be devastating. Ned fell quite often, the result leaving him a little wetter for the wear. Unfortunately, so it left some of the rocks. Clay didn't see it. He had managed fifteen in a row without batting an eyelash, which technically he didn't have; but on the sixteenth rock, he slipped. It happened so fast there was nothing he could do.

Ned splashed to his side. But Clay was already melting through his fingers. Clay's eyes, nose and mouth had disappeared. Ned salvaged what he could, drying Clay in his shirt, laying him down in a dry bed of moss.

With a twig, he poked eyes for his friend. "Clay?" he whispered, his voice shaking.

Clay stared up at him blankly.

Ned sliced Clay a mouth. Slowly, it curved into a tremulous smile.

"You're alive!" Ned cried.

Clay blinked his freshly poked eyes. "Parts of me disintegrated into oblivion," he said weakly.

"I'm just glad the real part didn't," said Ned.

The real part? What did Ned mean?

But Clay left the question unasked. The boy had cradled him in his arms, saying: "Let's get you back in shape and play something else."

So they did.

Even so, there was a new reality Clay couldn't escape – *he was clay.* And as great as summer was, it wouldn't last forever. And neither did boys, nor did their belief. Sooner or later, Clay would only be clay to Ned.

Fall would come. Then winter.

September was picking time. The work was time consuming. Days went by when the only moment Ned had for Clay was after supper. Some evenings, Ned was so tired he went straight to bed. On those nights, Clay would wait by the bridge and stay there until the telltale lantern light illumined Ned's upstairs window. Most nights, Ned remembered to look out and wave goodnight. Clay would wave back, waiting there until Ned's lantern light went out.

Then, Clay would cross the bridge, slink up the trees, and pick apples from the branches, leaving Father scratching his head at the fruit piled in pyramids on the ground the next morning. Unfortunately, Clay's time saving efforts only went so far. Picking was only part of the job. There was peeling and coring and mashing and baking and cleaning up afterward; not to mention the not so distant reality that when harvest season ended, Ned and his family would be heading to town and not returning until spring.

And winter was a long season for belief to endure.

As for the subject of belief, the two seemed to be avoiding it. Clay didn't know if the reason was that Ned was a boy and boys generally didn't think about such things, or if it was the fear that bringing up the matter might make the matter depart more quickly, or if it was simply the fact that belief is one of those subjects that is hard to talk about. For whatever reason, the topic remained unspoken but ever present like a shadow. It was the dark part that Clay couldn't shake and that would trail behind their time together.

The leaves changed color.

The last day of September was Ned and Clay's as well. Mother was wrapping jars in burlap and straw, Father was bridling the horse, and Betsy was hanging the laundry. Ned was sent to the creek to wash buckets, a chore which gave him the chance to steal a few final minutes to be with his friend.

It was their last moment together, and Clay was so full of emotion all he could manage to say was, "I'll miss you."

"Me, too," said Ned.

Then, Mother called and Ned disappeared up the tiny path his feet had made over many trips that summer. Brown leaves closed behind him.

You're better than I could have imagined.

An Unexpected Visit

CLAY COULDN'T BEAR to watch the Farmer family's horse cart bump away. Not even the hope it would return could soothe the painful sadness he felt. The adventures they would no longer share and the fear he couldn't shake that Ned would lose his belief sunk Clay deep into his deposit where he didn't move for days. In the past, such immobility would have been normal for Clay. But that summer had been so active, stagnation was a big change. And though change was Clay's nature, this one felt permanent.

The nights were cold. In the morning, Clay would be covered in a blanket of leaves. Some days the autumn wind brushed them off. Some days it didn't. Clay didn't bother with the leaves either way – not even the morning they crunched.

Clay felt the cold metal slide beneath him.

"I can't believe I'm doing this," said Ned's father, his feet crunching leaves while he shoveled Clay into a potato sack. "Sue is going to kill me."

(I should explain.)

What happened was this: Once Ned's family had settled back in town, Mr. Farmer had driven the horse cart back to the orchard in order to finish preparing the farm for winter. There were buckets, barrels, and tools to store; canvas tarpaulins to lash over the farm equipment; shutters to nail the windows shut and holes to fill in the floorboards. Basically, it took work to prepare a house for no one to be in it.

Clay crossed his mind only in the last instant.

That morning walking to the bridge, Mr. Farmer's eyes had fixed on something across the bank and past the orchard, a place that may have existed only between his ears when he was struck by a flood of nostalgia – of how much his son that summer had reminded him of the boy he used to be, and the realization that time had passed. He wasn't the same. And yet there was his boy playing in the same creek he once played. *Time had passed,* he thought, the creek flowing by, *so much so time had gone full circle.*

Why the thought compelled him to scoop Clay into a potato sack, he couldn't say. He didn't know. It was one of those spontaneous, intuitive decisions that end up affecting your life forever. Rarely do you recognize them when they happen. Sometimes not even in retrospect.

Clay was in the same boat, or horse cart rather, as he bounced on the boards with no idea where the journey would lead him…how could he?

How can any of us?

They made one stop along the way. Pulling the reins, Mr. Farmer laughed ironically as he left to return minutes later with a well-wrapped package that clinked beside Clay in his burlap sack. "Don't you break now, you hear?" Mr. Farmer said as the horse cart bumped along. "I'm going to need you to keep me on Mrs. Farmer's good side after she sees what else's back there."

Gifts

THE FARMERS LIVED in a town called Buena Vista, where Mule Lick Creek feeds into Brown River. It was a timeless looking place with cobblestone streets and a central square that boasted a redbrick church on one end and a brownstone municipal building on the other. The Farmers lived in a townhouse a few blocks from the square. It was a narrow, two-story home with a bricked-in backyard just like the others on the street.

Betsy and Ned were outside playing hopscotch on the road when the horse cart turned the corner. "Father!" they shouted, hugging his waist the moment it was in reach.

"Go on inside. I've got some things to show you," Father said with a smile.

"Gifts!" Betsy cried, clapping her hands.

"Oh boy!" shouted Ned.

Hearing the commotion, Mother appeared in the doorframe. "Children, you heard your Father. Wash up. Make sure you use soap, Ned," she called as the children breezed by.

Mr. Farmer climbed the stairs. "Sure nice to be home," he said, bowing to peck his wife on the cheek. "I got something for you, too," he added with a wink.

Mrs. Farmer blushed where the kiss had been while her husband took her arm. The door shut behind them.

Back in the horse cart, Clay climbed out of his potato sack, jumped off the horse cart and hurried to a window, which was open a crack.

"I paid a visit to the Potter," said Father, leading the family into the front room where he placed a knapsack on the table. "Now, we all know how upset Mother was when her favorite mixing bowl broke on our way down from the orchard. Well, last week on my way back up, I stopped by the Potter's to ask if he could make a new one." The children danced with anticipation. "Could he?" Father exclaimed. He held out his hands to demonstrate. "The Potter took a lump of clay, no different than the clay we have along Mule Lick Creek, and," he snapped his fingers, "just like that he made a bowl. It was magic. If I hadn't seen it with my own eyes, I wouldn't have believed it." He pulled back the flap on his knapsack.

The four family members leaned in. Clay stretched to get a better view.

"They're called nesting bowls," explained Father, handing the smallest of three to his wife. The bowl was white as milk with a hint of sapphire around the rim, like cloud and sky in the place they came together, perhaps why the bowl appeared to float in her hands. Tenderly, Mother placed it inside the others.

The nesting bowls were the most beautiful things Clay had ever seen.

"This is clay?" asked Betsy.

"Made of," said Father.

"How did it get so–"

"Perfect?" said Mother, finishing her daughter's question.

"Like I said, the man is a magician."

"I'd say," agreed Ned.

"They must have cost a fortune," said Mother.

"To tell the truth, I only purchased one," Father confessed, "but when I told the Potter that the bowl was intended for the woman responsible for *Mrs. Farmer's Famous Apple Butter*, he insisted I take all three. He's very fond of your apple butter. He told me to tell you so."

Mother's pink cheeks glowed. "Well, I will have to send him a jar for appreciation. As for you," she said, cupping her husband's cheeks, "you deserve a thank-you-kiss."

"I missed you," he said, looking into her eyes that had become moist like dew drops.

"We missed you, too," chimed Ned and Betsy.

Father laughed, "Then, it's unanimous!" He placed a hand on Betsy's head. "Let's see, what else do I have here? Ah yes," he said, rummaging. "One for you," handing a small wrapped item to Betsy, "and for you," placing a similar package in Ned's eager hands.

"What is it?" asked Betsy.

"Open and see," Father suggested.

Ned's wrapping paper was already torn to shreds. "Wow!" he exclaimed, examining the contents with a touch of awe. "It almost looks real."

"Real? What is it?" asked Betsy.

"See for yourself," said Ned, holding out the ceramic figurine.

Again, Clay maneuvered to gain perspective.

"Is it alive?" she asked.

"It's clay," explained Father.

"That's not clay. That's a frog," she said, crinkling her nose.

"Ribbit," croaked Ned.

Betsy jumped.

"Don't be frightened. Your brother's just pretending," said Father.

"That frog sure doesn't look pretend."

"Ribbit," croaked Ned, hopping the figurine toward his sister.

"That's enough, young man," said Mother, cringing. "Pretend or not, I don't want you scaring your sister with it. Or anyone else for that matter."

Ned frowned.

"Thank you," said Mother.

"Can I go to my room?" he asked. "I want to find a place for it."

"Sure, Son," said Father, "but don't you want to see what the Potter made your sister?"

"Oh yeah," said Ned. "Go on, Sis. Maybe it's a butterfly. Frogs eat butterflies, I think."

"Not this one," she said, guarding her package with her hands.

As it turned out, the object was not a figurine. It was a box meant for jewelry. The lid fit so perfectly it was almost seamless. On top, the knob was fashioned to look like a bouquet of roses – purple, red, pink, and white. Stems came down to mark the corners. Each traveled down the side to the base where they curled to spirals that served as the box's feet.

Clay changed his mind. *This* was the most beautiful thing he had ever seen.

"How did the Potter know that roses were my favorite flower? Did you tell him, Father?"

"They were wrapped when I arrived," he said in wonderment – also to explain to his wife why the beautiful box was not for her.

"It's too…" Mother began, but before she finished it was as if something came over her, for she said, "Come Elizabeth [which was the name she called Betsy], let's find something special to put inside," whispering, "I think I know just the thing."

Betsy brightened. Mother traced the back of her daughter's head with her hand. In the twinkle of an eye, the two skipped out of sight.

"Can I go to my room now, Father?" asked Ned.

"Yes," he said.

"Ribbit," croaked Ned, hopping to the stairs.

Father found a seat in the suddenly quiet room. Leaning back, he laced his calloused fingers behind his ears and looked very pleased with himself. The surprise in the burlap potato sack could wait until morning.

Heart Break

"WHAT IS IT?" asked Ned after breakfast.

"If I told you, it wouldn't be a surprise," answered Father. He lowered his voice and looked both ways. "It's outside, wrapped in burlap. Now, do me a favor, and don't tell Mother about it." At that, Ned's heart burped. A present Mother wasn't allowed to know about – that was something!

He was outside without tying his shoelaces.

"Clay!" he cried, peeling the sack open.

Clay blinked two poked eyes.

"You're here!" Ned cheered. "I can't believe it!"

"Me, too," said Clay, grinning from ear to cockeyed ear, because the thing they couldn't believe wasn't the kind of thing Clay needed to worry about.

"I've got so much to tell you," he said, pulling down the sides of the potato sack and bending Clay's elbow loose. "Father brought pottery home. He said it came from clay just like you. Was it? Was it from you?"

Clay shook his head.

"I didn't think so. I'm –" But Ned was interrupted before he could finish his thought.

"What're you talking to?" came the gravelly voice of Guinevere Sprout.

Ned took a deep breath before turning around.

"Gwen" had red curly hair and wore a smudge on her face that was really a birthmark, and if you said anything about it, she'd punch you. She was nine, two years older than Ned, and to him, she was equal parts terror and attraction. Ned couldn't help being enthralled by her zest for mischief, not to mention her age and the stunning wildness of her hair, which combined to make Gwen about the prettiest human being that ever paid Ned a lick of attention.

A boy named Billy was with her. He lived down the block in a townhouse on the right. He had small eyes, profuse freckles and muscles above his elbows. He was nine, too, and dead set on making sure Ned knew he was inferior. Especially when Gwen was around.

Ned feared him. He feared both of them. At the same time, he wanted their approval desperately, so much so that, despite the part of Ned that knew better, the last few weeks he had done whatever these two hooligans asked of him. A pleasant arrangement for Gwen and Billy, they rather enjoyed telling others what to do.

(You may see where this is going.)

So when Gwen interrupted Ned and Clay's reunion, asking: "What're you talking to?" Ned's insides tensed and he said, "Nothing," uncertain what good would come from her knowing the truth. Vainly, he tried to conceal Clay by lifting the burlap behind him.

"Looks like something to me," said Billy, stopping his arm.

"It's just clay," said Ned. The way he said *clay* wasn't the way he usually said it.

"Let me see," said Gwen, shoving Ned and Billy aside. "Hey, it's a little person!"

Clay didn't budge.

"Is this your imaginary friend?" asked Billy.

"He doesn't look imaginary to me," said Gwen. She licked her cracked lips. "I think Neddy thinks he's real."

"No, I don't!" said Ned. His heart clenched.

"Of course he is," said Gwen. "Look, he's got eyes and a mouth."

"Ned drew them there," said Billy.

"No, he didn't. This little fella must have come from the hill country for a visit. Didn'tcha, little fella?" She punched Clay in the arm. "Didn'tcha?" She punched him so hard the arm came off.

Ned's voice caught in his throat.

"You hurt him," said Billy, picking up Clay's dismembered arm. "Here you go, little fella," swinging the arm like a bat. It wrapped around Clay's body like a crowbar.

"Stop!" shouted Ned, unable to contain the horror.

"What's wrong, Neddy?" Billy asked with innocent malevolence.

"Won't you share your friend with us?" asked Gwen, batting her eyelashes.

Ned fought back the shaking, the tears welling in his eyes, the twisting in his heart. His hands went to fists. Then, with a horrendous scream he punched Clay square on the nose.

"How cute!" said Gwen, inspecting. "You can see tiny finger marks." She socked Ned in the arm. "Nice shot."

Ned smiled, the warmth radiating from the spot she had hit him. Trembling, he punched Clay again; this time in the stomach; then on the shoulder, then in the chest – straight to the heart that Clay technically didn't have. The one that was breaking.

"Hey," said Billy, "let's use the little fella for target practice. We can draw a bulls-eye right here." Pulling out a penknife, he carved a circle on Clay's wounded torso.

"We already know who's got the best aim," said Gwen with a flip to her curly hair.

"We'll see about that," said Billy. "There's plenty rocks by the river."

"What do you say, Clay?" she said, patting the disfigured glob like a stray pet.

Tears streamed down Ned's face. He was ashamed at what he had done. He was embarrassed he was crying.

"What do you say, Ned?" Gwen asked, putting her arm around the boy. "You want to play with us, don't you?"

Ned wiped his running nose with his forearm. He smeared the tears off his cheeks. "What do I care?" he said, "It's just a lump of clay."

When they were finished, Clay was nothing more than a mangled mess of stones, boot prints and swords made from branches. They left him by the river like a discarded piece of trash.

Gwen walked Ned to his house. "You're tough, kid," she said. It was like she was pinning on a medal. Ned could feel the needle prick. It pierced his heart.

He couldn't wait to get home – couldn't wait for the spanking he hoped Mother would give him for how filthy he'd become; or better, one from his Father for all the trouble he went through to bring Clay only for his son to destroy him. He doubted Clay could ever forgive him. He doubted Clay even existed anymore.

He wouldn't to Ned, not after what he had done. Clay was gone – and part of Ned was gone, too. Still, silently, as Ned walked toward the punishment he prayed would come, he vowed that afterward he would go to the river and salvage what he could of his old friend.

But the punishment never came, not the kind Ned was hoping for. And when Ned returned to the river, Clay was no longer there.

Murder

TO HIS SURPRISE, Clay was able to reform quite easily. All the punching, poking, mashing, kicking, stabbing, smashing and pounding had actually made him stronger. If only strength translated to feelings. For he could do nothing about the stones, boot prints and branches that were sticking out here, there and everywhere like reminders. The truth was Clay was a mess through and through.

In the small difference between an open hand and a clenched fist, Ned had dashed his friend to pieces. Disappointment, confusion, betrayal – these were the fragments Clay found himself standing. They put a slump to his shoulder that no reshaping could alter.

"Well, look who it is," cackled a familiar caw.

"Can't say we didn't warn you," crowed Craw.

Crick and Craw were perched with several of their friends (which is called a *murder,* believe it or not). They were cackling. The murder was cackling.

"I'm. I," Clay stuttered. "I'll be going now," he said, stretching his mangled legs.

Crick and Craw dropped to the ground to block Clay's path.

"Excuse me, please," Clay continued, moving to the side.

"Not so fast there, Lumpy," cawed Crick. "Where are you going?"

"To the Potter," said Clay, the thought suddenly coming to him.

"Why on earth would you do that?" crowed Craw.

"To be made," said Clay. It was an idea that was still forming.

Crick cackled, "Killed is more like it," pointing his beak like a dagger. "Don't you know what the Potter does to clay?"

Clay shrugged his sagging shoulders. The truth was he didn't know.

"First, he tortures it; then, he throws it in the fire. You know what happens next, don't you?"

"But," argued Clay. But who was he defending? What if the crows were right?

"If I were clay, the Potter'd be the last person on earth I'd go to see."

"But people cherish the things he makes," said Clay.

At that, the murder cackled so hard they rattled the branches. The clatter sounded like hollow bones.

Above them, the world had turned an unfeeling gray. A third crow dropped to the ground. She was missing an eye; in its place was a festering scab. "People are foolish," she rasped. "A bigger fool gets his value from people."

"But the Potter gives clay purpose," Clay explained, not entirely sure what he was saying.

"Purpose! What do you need a purpose for?" cawed Craw. Then, turning to his fellows: "Do you hear that, chaps? Clay wants purpose."

The murder laughed again.

"Let me level with you," Crick crowed, "purpose is overrated."

"You get a purpose, all the sudden you have responsibility," agreed the One-Eye crow.

"Right now, you're as free as a bird." Crick flapped his wings. "The minute you get purpose, you're not free anymore."

"Who in their right mind would trade freedom for purpose?" asked Craw.

"I don't know. Maybe Clay is crazy," cawed Crick.

"Tell me something I don't know," cackled Craw.

"Crazy as a canary," cackled Crick.

"Come all this way just to get thrown in the fire," crowed Craw.

"Brave the cold just to get himself burned!" cackled Crick.

"You're lying!" shouted Clay.

The murder of crows cackled in unison. The cold sound sent chills through Clay.

"Come on, chaps, let's show this fellow what it's like to fly," Craw cawed.

The murder rattled the branches.

"Wait!" called Clay. "Does the Potter really do those things you say?"

The crows swooped in a wide circle. Only One-Eye remained. "Trust me," she rasped. "All purpose gives you is pain, suffering, and death."

"But what if I was meant to be made," said Clay.

"Why on earth would you think that?" asked One-Eye.

"Sometimes I wonder if there's more to life than just being Clay."

"You are Clay," crowed One-Eye.

"But I've seen made things," Clay stammered. "They are beautiful."

"Beauty comes at a price." A dark spark flashed in the crow's marble eye.

"What price?" asked Clay.

"Pain," she crowed. "Beauty is pain."

"I'll pay," said Clay.

One-Eye cackled. "What do you have to offer?"

Clay didn't know.

She ruffled her feathers. "Look, if you won't listen to me, ask made things what it's like. Maybe they can talk sense into you."

"Where are these made things?" asked Clay.

"Do I really need to answer that?" cawed One-Eye.

"In town?" Clay asked timidly.

"Made things are everywhere," she cawed. "Getting them to speak is the tricky part." One-Eye stretched her wings.

"What do you mean get them to speak?" asked Clay.

But the crow with the missing eye had risen to join the murder. They had roosted across the river in the barren branches lining the roadside. They were mocking a horse that was pulling a cart over the bumps. Clay could hear their raucous laughter.

"What do they know?" Clay muttered, turning back to the town of Buena Vista. "What do I know either?" he whispered. His thoughts drifted to the scene he witnessed yesterday by the window: the delight that came over Mother as she caressed the nesting bowls, the joy that bubbled out of Ned at the sight of his frog figurine, the awe they shared at the beauty of Betsy's jewelry box, the look of satisfaction on Father's face as he laced his hands behind his head – it all happened because of clay like him.

Made things were treasured.

What if he was made? Would he be treasured, too?

All of a sudden, it was like the universe – every star, solar system, galaxy, and the space between them – filled every mineral and molecule of Clay with energy. All those nights he spent wondering if there was more to life than being Clay – what if there was? What if there was something he was *meant* to become? What if a purpose was the thing he was missing? Was that the answer? Yes. Purpose. It had to be. "It must be," he sighed quietly to himself.

"I'll never be hurt again," he said, at once hopeful and sad. For a move toward meaning felt like a break with the past, with his friend, the one who had hurt him. The one he still loved. It was too painful to think about. *Better to look forward* he encouraged himself to think. Perhaps, one day, as a made thing, somebody would accept Clay like a treasure. No, not Clay. Clay would be something else. "Something wonderful, I hope."

He whistled, the note melting into what sounded like a *dong*.

Dong? Smooth and melancholy, it was the *dong* of a bell. Over there in the center of town, swinging back and forth like Ned's legs off the branch of the old oak tree: *a bell that someone made*. It was attached to a pulley that was attached to a tower that was attached to a building in a town full of made things.

One-Eye was right. Made things were everywhere. Perhaps her advice about talking to them was right, too. At least they could tell him the truth about the Potter. But what did she mean about getting them to speak?

Part Two —
Made Things

Imagine the possibility of being magnificent like this.

Getting Things
to Speak

WITH FRESH DETERMINATION, Clay placed his feet on the thin dirt path leading back to town. Cottages cropped up along either side until the dirt transitioned to cobblestones and the grassy yards changed to the porch stoops of townhouses. The houses lined the street with windows low enough Clay could see through them, so long as the curtains weren't drawn.

A family was having supper around a table. At one end, the lady of the house was pouring tea into cups. She passed them to her family, two sons and a husband. Clay recognized one of the boys. His hair was combed and his face was pouting, but it was the same

Billy that had earlier used his body for target practice. The sight made Clay recoil. But just as he was about to retreat from the window, the lady of the house gathered the final tea-cup in her hands. Her fingertips went pink. Her lips spread in a grin while the lines in her face relaxed. It was like the strands of steam were lifting the burdens right out of her.

Now that was a purpose, Clay thought. *I'll have to ask a cup what it's like to be held like that.*

Just then, One-Eye's warning about getting things to speak came to mind. It made sense, finally. How could a teacup talk without a mouth?

Something *hissed* in the shadows.

"What was that?" Clay cried, jumping back.

Psssst the Something hissed again.

"Who's there?" asked Clay, looking around.

Us, the Hisser said.

"Who's us?"

We are.

"Who...where are you?" Clay asked.

Here.

"Where's here?"

Where we are.

"Where is that?"

Here.

"Look," said Clay, getting frustrated, "I need a little more direction."

That's why we're talking to you, said the voice.

"Who?" spluttered Clay.

Us.

"What's your name?" he asked the invisible stranger.

Brick, the voice replied.

Clay took another step back. "You mean the bricks on the house?"

Where else would we be?

Clay must have been hearing things. How could a brick talk? Maybe the crows were right. Maybe he *was* crazy.

There's more than one way to talk, Brick explained.

"What did you say?" asked Clay.

You wondered how bricks could talk. I answered for us. To be honest, talking is not the challenge. It's the listening that makes it hard to hear.

Slowly, Clay approached the side of the building where the voice was coming from. Did the bricks on the wall just read his thoughts?

Yes, said Brick, *and we might add that you are reading our thoughts, too.*

But I never read a thought in my life, thought Clay.

Of course you have, Brick replied. *But now is not the time to go into such things. We're talking to you because you have questions about being made.*

"You know?" asked Clay, still coming to grips with the fact he was talking to a wall.

Once upon a time we were clay like you.

"You were clay?"

Red clay to be exact. We're found in abundance down river. You look more like brownstone, which is usually from the hill country.

"I am from the hill country," said Clay, surprised.

There you are, said Brick.

"Which brick are you?" asked Clay, leaning closer.

Three bricks to the right of the corner, eleven from the bottom.

Clay counted, but keeping Brick separate from the others was no easy task. "Hello?" said Clay, squinting.

Hello, Brick replied.

"Can all of you speak?"

Of course. But it isn't necessary since we would all tell you the same thing.

Clay didn't understand why Brick kept saying *we* and *us* instead of *I* and *me*. Maybe it was the way clay talked down river.

I say we, answered Brick, reading Clay's thoughts, *because once I became part of this building, I became more than myself.*

"What does that mean?"

We individual bricks have become one building. Together, we are greater than what we were when apart.

"And before you were bricks you were clay?" asked Clay.

In a sense we still are. We are a building made of bricks made from clay.

"But you cannot move."

Precisely. Immovability happens to be one of our greatest assets.

Clay would have to think about that.

Tell me, what's so great about movement?

"It's useful," Clay said without conviction.

How useful is clay against the rain?

Not very, thought Clay.

How well does clay keep things clean?

Not well at all, thought Clay.

Maybe you are not as useful as you think you are, said Brick. *Don't take it personally. There are wonderful things about clay. But if you want to be made, it's going to cost your flexibility.* Brick paused to let the words sink in. *To become a brick, we had to give up our ability to change shape. It was a sacrifice but one worth the taking.*

Clay hadn't thought about sacrifice. Madeness would give him certain qualities but cost him others. Perhaps that was the price One-Eye was talking about. Clay's mind wandered down the cobblestone street to the impressive exterior of the bell tower. He looked back at the simple townhouse before him. He wondered if Brick ever regretted being part of something less distinguished.

That was another sacrifice, answered Brick, reading Clay's thoughts again. *When we became part of this building, we gave up the possibility of becoming part of another.* Brick paused. *The Buena Vista Bell Tower is very impressive. Many important things happen inside their walls, but we Bricks get the special honor of housing a family. And it's hard to imagine a purpose better than that. That's what you want, right? A purpose?*

Clay didn't know what to say even though he was quite certain that he wanted a purpose very badly.

Brownstone makes beautiful buildings. The Buena Vista Bell Tower is made of it.

"The bell tower is made of brownstone like me?" Clay brightened.

Long ago, those brownstone blocks were clay like you. But over time they became hard.

"Could that happen to me?" Clay asked.

Yes. But it would take a very long time.

"But if it happened," continued Clay, "could I be part of a magnificent building like the bell tower?"

Brick didn't reply right away, and when Brick did, Brick seemed to be changing the subject: *The great thing about clay is that it can be made into most anything.*

"So it's possible to become a brick."

Many things are in the realm of possibility.

"Including being made into a brick," Clay asserted.

Including being made into a brick, said Brick.

Clay hid his twiddling thumbs behind his back. "Do you think the Buena Vista Bell Tower might talk to me?"

Hard to say. No two buildings are exactly alike.

Clay would have liked more assurance.

We hope you find what you're looking for.

"Thanks." Clay sidestepped toward the center of town. "And thanks for talking to me."

Thanks for listening, all the Bricks said at once.

The cobblestones quivered under Clay's feet. "Wow, you sure have a lot of volume! Is that why you use a spokesman?"

There's a reason for everything, said Brick.

"I guess there is. Thanks again," said Clay, "I'll be seeing you."

You know where to find us, said Brick. *We're not going anywhere.*

The Shadow
of Dignity

THE BUENA VISTA Bell Tower was even more impressive up close. Its chiseled blocks fit together so perfectly they rose from the earth like a single formation. In the moonlight, Clay couldn't fully appreciate the façade's spectacular reddish, purplish hue, but its purpose was not lost on him. This was power. This was authority. This was greatness by accumulation.

People called it a municipal building. Besides tolling the time, the Bell Tower housed books, meetings, and even a jail. Clay knew none of this; still, the structure awed and intimidated him. At the same time, he was unable to resist the urge to touch and feel what clay like him had become, to imagine the possibility of being magnificent like this. It seemed better than a dream, and he placed a clay hand on the nearest block as if to make sure it wasn't one.

The brownstone was cold, proud.

Excuse you, quaked a voice that shook the ground beneath Clay's feet.

"Excuse me," said Clay, removing his hand like a caught child.

What do you think you are doing? The brownstone blocks were very dignified.

Clay took a few steps back to give such dignity its space.

So you are wondering what it is like to be so important.

"Yes sirs," said Clay.

One sir will do.

"Yes, Sir Brownstone," said Clay, bowing slightly. "Are you from the hill country?"

Sir Brownstone scoffed. *No hill around here. We were extracted from Hummelstown.*

"Where is that?" asked Clay.

Where is that? Only the most prestigious quarry in the world!

"Oh, yes, of course," said Clay.

Of all the brownstone in Hummelstown Quarry, we were the chosen – hewn from boulders, chiseled to blocks, transported by train, assembled by masons.

"Pardon me for asking, Sir, but what's a mason?"

Masons are men who build with stone and mortar. A master mason constructed us.

"Where do you find these masons?"

What would you want with a mason? scoffed Sir Brownstone.

Clay shrugged his shoulders. "Maybe one could make me part of a magnificent building."

You! exclaimed Sir Brownstone. *You are clay.*

Clay didn't get the impression Sir Brownstone was paying him a compliment.

You would be better off with a potter. That is about all clay is good for.

"But weren't you once clay like me?" asked Clay.

That was a very long time ago. And we do not recall ever being clay like you.

"What do you mean?"

Look at you: twigs and stones sticking out here, there and everywhere. What a mess! A disgrace to the Brownstone name. In all our existence, we have never seen such rubbish. You'd be lucky if the

Potter doesn't take you to the dump the moment he lays eyes on you. As far as we can see (and we can see a long way) that is precisely where you will land in the end.

"But I thought that maybe I was supposed to become something," whimpered Clay.

Not all things are meant to become something. Some clay is meant to be clay.

"You're lying!"

We most certainly are not!

Clay could not believe his ears. Of course he was meant to become something. Anger knotted his insides like a rat nest. His eyes shrank to nail holes of fury. Sir Brownstone on the other hand was rigid, emotionless, and incapable of feeling. They certainly did not care about Clay's.

"Well, I know one thing, Mr. Sir Brownstone Bell Tower," stammered Clay, "I know I don't want to become part of a building like you."

Good. Then we are in agreement.

"Agreement?" asked Clay, confused.

We agree that we do not want you to become part of a building like us.

Clay kicked Sir Brownstone in the cornerstone. His foot lodged.

Get off of me, you piece of dirt!

"I'm trying," said Clay, tugging so hard he fell to the cobblestones.

You left a smudge, cried Sir Brownstone indignantly.

At that, Clay muttered a few words more becoming of mud.

If being made is so important to you, make yourself into a mud pie.

Clay did not have a response for that.

Do you have something to say? asked Sir Brownstone.

"No," grumbled Clay.

Then, good-bye and good riddance.

"I'll be made. You wait and see," Clay said, shaking a fist.

Sir Brownstone was stone-faced, stark and distant.

Bombs Away

DEFEATED, CLAY TRUDGED into the night, a nameless weight slouching his shoulders into a sad and lonely hunch. He slumped through town with no purpose whatsoever, every step taking effort. While above him, clouds gathered. There weren't even stars to keep him company tonight.

By morning, the overcast sky hung heavy with rain. It was drizzling now – not enough to disintegrate Clay, but enough to make him cling to everything he touched. With each step there was a little less of him.

"Look at me," he muttered, "sticks and stones sticking out here, there, and every-where. Drizzle turning my slip to slop. What a mess. What a disgrace." He plodded down the cobblestones.

A man in a long coat stepped out of his house, took one look at Clay, gasped: "Dear heavens, what is that?" and splashed down the street shielding himself with his umbrella.

The drizzle turned to rain.

Escaping down an alley, Clay ducked into a brick portico, retreated to the door and squatted to his haunches. A few feet away, rain tinkled on the street like a polite applause. It dripped from the portico's arched canopy. Across the alleyway, ivy clung in tendrils to a brick wall. There was an iron gate, a table with an umbrella in the yard. A lady was sitting with an object in her hands. Steam drifted from the object like a peace offering – the warm welcome of a morning cup of tea – when suddenly a *crash* came from inside the house. It was the kind of noise that happened just before Ned received a scolding.

"Billy, stop harassing your little brother!" the lady of the house yelled. "Johnny, stop asking for it!"

Another crash.

The lady of the house placed the teacup on the table: "Don't make me come in there!"

One of the boys started crying.

"I didn't do it," cried the brother.

The lady dabbed the corners of her mouth with a napkin. Then, brushing the crumbs off her dress, she tip-toed through the rain, climbed the stairs and slammed the door behind her.

Breakfast was over. The teacup was alone.

This was Clay's chance. There was only one problem: the weather that had been tinkling like a polite applause had turned into a standing ovation. Rain exploded on the ground like bombshells. Puddles dotted the yard like landmines. Droplets clung to the grass like poison-dipped spears. In such a minefield, Clay couldn't survive.

But the moment the rain stopped, the lady would return.

Hey you, said a Brick halfway up the doorframe.

"Me?" said Clay, turning upward.

Look. You go out in weather like this, and you'll melt into oblivion.

"But I need to talk to that teacup," said Clay.

Course you do, said Brick. *So here's what you're going to do.*

Whoa, whoa, whoa, said an Other Brick. *Don't listen to One. He's nuts.*

It appeared these Bricks were not as unified as the ones across the street.

Quiet, I'm talking, retorted One. *Now, listen here. You see that piece of paper hanging from that tack on the door? It's called a Public Notice. I read it. It's meaningless. But not for you, see – that Notice is gonna be your ticket.*

Suddenly, Clay understood. Stretching his arm, he ripped the paper from the tack.

Don't! cried The Other. *You'll melt into oblivion!*

But Clay's mind was made up. Forming into a miniature version of himself, he spread the Public Notice above his head like an umbrella. Then, taking a deep breath, he hopped to the street, dodged puddles, slipped through the gate and disappeared beneath an azalea, leaving the rest-of-him behind.

Through the leaves, Clay measured the remaining distance and sighed. There was no way across. His feet had eroded to the ankles. His fingers had melted into mittens. And the Public Notice had disintegrated to a pulp.

A raindrop landed on Clay's head like a warning shot. The droplet streaked down his cheek like a tear, taking a bit of him with it. Time was running out in more ways than one. It was dissolving away like sand from an hourglass, like mud into a river.

Clay slopped to the ivy by the wall. The vines were a tangle of yarn, glistening like wet wax. But to his surprise, the undersides were dry. Clay tugged the nearest. It didn't budge. A few rain-bombs fell, but Clay managed to avoid them.

He placed his foot on the vine. Taking hold, he moved upward. His head grazed the back of the ivy, but the back was dry. He stepped higher.

Higher. With every inch he gained ground... gained optimism. Higher he climbed... higher...

An idea was taking form. He was working out the details.

That's the spirit! cheered Bricks.

You can do it! cheered others.

"Thanks for the vote of confidence," said Clay, continuing up.

Just don't look down, they said.

Which, of course, Clay did, the sight filling his every mineral and molecule with terror. All of a sudden, Clay didn't feel so optimistic.

Especially when the vine in his right hand snapped!

Rain-shrapnel cascaded down.

Clay grasped. But there was nothing to grasp. His right foot sheared off. He lost balance. His left foot skated on the branches as if they were made of ice. He dangled by a hand, a wet one that was losing grip.

Bricks *screamed*, which didn't help.

Desperately, Clay lunged for another hand-hold, but the vine was out of reach. He could stretch his arm, but then it would be too weak to hold his weight.

He slipped to fingertips.

He made the mistake of looking down again. He gulped. But just then, something caught his eye, something in his chest. A twig. Quickly, Clay dislodged the debris with his right hand. He jammed it in a crack between two bricks just as his left hand gave way.

Bricks *gasped.*

Clay swung.

Bricks *held their breath.*

Clay held on. His feet found a dry vine.

Bricks *cheered.*

Clay heaved a deep sigh of relief. "Who would have thought my mess would come in so handy?" he said, once his heart, which he technically didn't have, stopped thumping in his throat.

"Thanks for being so sturdy," he said to the bricks the twig was between.

Don't mention it, they said.

Clay found a handhold. Carefully, he climbed the rest of the way to the top. "Now, the real adventure begins," he whispered.

From the ground, Clay had noticed that the umbrella had a rope around its fringe. If he jumped from the wall, landed on the umbrella, slid to the edge, grabbed the rope and swung to the table – instead of splat, he might go plop. That was the idea.

From his current position, it didn't seem like much of one.

Beads of water raced down the canvas umbrella. They skydived to the brick patio and exploded. Clay imagined following the same route. What he imagined didn't feel so good, especially the explosion part.

Don't give up, Clay, whispered the Brick underneath him.

There are worse things than going splat, encouraged another.

Like what? Clay wondered.

Brick didn't say.

A rogue raindrop sliced off his ear. It was now or never. Turning back wasn't an option. Besides, this was his chance to talk to the tea-cup.

"Here goes nothing...everything," he whispered, brushing ivy to the side.

He took a deep breath, let out a whistle.

And jumped.

The most beautiful word in the history of words.

China

NOW THAT'S WHAT I call an entrance, said the teacup. Her voice was like wind chimes. *I knew you could do it.*

"Knew?" Clay said, looking up from the wad he had become. Truth be told, he was amazed there was any Clay left. Flying through the air, Clay was convinced he had just committed the most foolish act of his existence (as well as his last). However, miraculously he had landed on the umbrella, slid to the fringe, gripped the rope, flipped around, performed two unintentional somersaults and plopped smack dab in the middle of a crumb-covered plate.

I hoped you would, she said.

"Hoped?"

Yes, she said. *Hope is the gift we're given while we wait.*

"Gift?"

Do you always speak in one word responses?
she asked, giggling.

He almost said "No," but that would have
been another one word response.

The fact was Clay couldn't stop staring at
her. Teacup was so simple yet *so beautiful*. She
was white as milk with a rim like a halo of
gold. But what astounded Clay most was how
thin she was – so much thinner than Clay
dared become, yet there was no doubt she
was stronger than Clay had ever been.

Are you all right? asked Teacup.

"Huh?" uttered Clay, lost in the slender
curve of her handle.

You don't look so well.

"Oh," he said, noticing for the first time
the shape he was in. Embarrassed, Clay hastily
reformed into an even mini-er mini version of
his human-like form.

Teacup giggled again. The sound reminded
Clay of the music the water made sometimes
along Mule Lick Creek.

"Were you once clay?" he asked bashfully.

Of course, she said.

"And now you're a cup?"

At your service.

"What's your name?"

China. The way she said it, *China* sounded like the most beautiful word in the history of words.

"That's beautiful," said Clay.

Thank you, she said as if she were blushing.

"When were you made?" he asked.

Not long ago, she answered before adding, *the Potter made me.*

Clay leaned forward. "You know the Potter?"

Would you like me to tell you about him?

Clay didn't reply.

What a silly question! Of course you would. He's the reason you came.

Was he? Clay was finding it difficult to remember when all of a sudden the reason came to him – the murder of crows – the things they said about what the Potter did to clay. It angered him to think that the Potter did those things to China.

You don't understand, said China, reading his mind.

"The Potter beat you? He put you in fire?" The mere thought boiled Clay's insides.

Yes, she replied. *What you heard about the Potter is factual. But there is a difference sometimes between fact and truth.*

"What do you mean?"

You already know. You are clay. It's what happens to us.

"But I haven't met the Potter."

But you have been shaped.

"Shaped?"

Cut, mashed, thrown, punched, poked, pounded, beaten...pick your word for it. I like shaped. Don't act surprised, Clay. It's not like you haven't been shaped before.

Clay's eyes grew wide. She was right. He experienced almost every one of those words each day. Shaping wasn't bad; shaping was life. So why did it sound so awful the way the crows described it?

They're not clay, replied China, reading his thoughts. *In fact, the more you are punched, poked and pounded –*

"The stronger I become," finished Clay. He knew. He was clay.

The difference is that when the world does it to you, the results can be rather messy.

Clay wondered if she was using his current condition as an example.

The Potter is different. The process might feel the same, but his results are good.

"But what about fire?" asked Clay. "I understand what you're saying about being shaped, but fire sounds dangerous."

Fire is dangerous if you value your current condition.

"You don't? I mean, you didn't?"

It wasn't too long ago that I was clay like you. Not brownstone. I am kaolin. The Potter dug me up from a deposit; he wheelbarrowed me to his cottage. There, he added a mixture of bone ash and feldspar. Then, he placed me under a cloth until he was ready.

"Did you have a say in the matter?" Clay asked.

What do you mean? asked China.

"Did you tell him what you wanted to be made into?"

No, she said, *that would be foolish.*

"Why?"

Do you know what you want to be made into?

"No," Clay admitted.

See? How was I to know what it meant to be a cup?

"But you wanted a purpose, didn't you?"

We all do, she said.

"So is being a cup enough?" Clay wasn't sure why he was getting upset, but he was.

It's what I am, China replied.

"Do you ever wish for more?"

What more could I want? I am cherished; I fill a need. What else is there?

"But you're just a cup. There are so many of you."

It's true I have brothers and sisters. Of course when my lady chooses me, I am the only one.

Clay didn't think he was getting through: "Don't you see? There are lots of things – made things – that clay can become. Some are more valuable than you."

Depending on what you value.

"Exactly! From what I understand some made things are very valuable. Other made things are worth less. Doesn't that bother you?" Clay hadn't thought about it until now, but the thought really bothered him.

I can only speak for myself, Clay. I'm content with who I am.

This conversation was getting more frustrating by the minute.

Don't get frustrated, she said.

"Stop reading my thoughts!" he yelled.

I'm sorry. It's just that before you go through it there is only so much you can understand. You are Clay.

"Thanks for reminding me," he muttered.

Just because I am made doesn't make me better than you.

Yes it does, thought Clay, looking away. The rain had stopped. Sunlight broke through the clouds, but Clay's world remained overcast.

I'm afraid we don't have much time. Soon, my lady will be coming to retrieve me. China sighed. *Oh, there's so much I want to tell you.*

"Like what? Like how great it is to be a cup," moaned Clay.

No, about beauty and worth...and the Potter.

"What?" he grumbled.

Well for one, you can trust him. You may doubt at times that he has your best interest in mind. But he does. You'll see, Clay. He won't let you down.

Clay sensed that China had his best interest in mind as well. The knowledge softened him, not physically, but on the inside. "I'm," he started, finding the words difficult. "I'm sorry, China, that I got frustrated."

Oh Clay, I'm the sorry one. I want so badly to help you, and I'm afraid I'm not doing a very good job.

Clay was about to tell her it was OK but a door slammed. Judging by the force, it didn't sound like the lady of the house was inclined to offer a blob of mud hospitality. So leaping to a chair, Clay used the table leg like a fireman's pole and slid to the ground. Above him, the lady of the house placed China on a muddy, crumb-filled plate.

Good-bye, Clay. Good luck on your journey, called China.

"Thank you," Clay called back. "Maybe we will meet again."

One can always hope, she said as she disappeared into the house.

"Can't wait," he said, watching the door close. And with that, Clay dodged puddles to the portico –

One to The Other

– STRAIGHT INTO a heated discussion:

Seriously, if you had to do it all over again, you would become a Brick, said One.

You ever see a sculpture made of red clay? asked The Other.

Give me a reason why red clay can't become a sculpture, replied One.

We make good bricks, said The Other.

Let someone else do the job. One wishes to be a sculpture.

You're a brick! exclaimed The Other.

One can dream.

What's the point? You're a brick!

Thanks a lot, Dreamkiller.

Just telling it like it is, said The Other.

Can't you see I wasn't talking about me? shouted One. *You listening, sonny?*

"Who, me?" asked Clay, having massaged himself into the rest-of-himself.

You're the only thing around here who's got potential.

Don't listen to One. He's just mad because he was chopped in half in order to fit.

Better One than The Other, said One.

Ha. Ha, said The Other.

All I'm saying is that Clay still has options. I'm putting myself in his position.

And what I'm saying is stop muddying the waters.

I'm not muddying waters; I'm offering advice, said One.

For heaven's sake what for? You know as well as I do that the Potter knows best.

"You know the Potter?" interjected Clay.

Not personally, said The Other. *We were made down river.*

"Oh."

But we know what we're talking about.

It's true, said The Other. *We've seen his handiwork. Tell him, One.*

Why don't you try not being so bossy? One doesn't appreciate being told what to do. But, seeing as I was about to tell him anyway. One paused. *Just don't think I'm telling him because you told me to.* One cleared his voice. *Excuse me. Now, where was I? Oh yeah, the Potter. Well, it so happens that the man who lives in us gave one of the Potter's pieces of artwork to his lady-friend last Christmas.*

"Really?"

Yes really. You think I'm making this up? He bought it from the gallery in the square.

"You mean the square where the Buena Vista Bell Tower is?" asked Clay.

Yes I mean that square. How many squares do you think a town has? asked One gruffly.

"Sorry. This is the only town I have ever seen."

My point exactly. You have options. You could travel the world if you want.

"I don't want to travel," said Clay. "I want to be made."

Well, that's easy. Go to the Potter and have him make you, said The Other.

Hold on! What if the Potter makes him into a chamber pot?

There's no shame in being a chamber pot. It's an important job.

How would you like to be urinated upon! exclaimed One.

It happened to me, said a brick lower to the ground, *it's not that fun.*

See? said One.

Be quiet, said The Other. *Look, the chances Clay will be made into a chamber pot are slim. People are using indoor plumbing nowadays.*

It'll never catch on, said One. *All I am saying is that the Potter might want some input. After all, Clay here will have to live with the results for a very long time.*

You really think the Potter cares about what clay has to say? asked The Other.

I would hope so. What kind of potter would he be if he didn't treat clay with a little respect?

I don't know, said The Other. *Maybe you're right.*

Of course I am.

All this time, Clay listened not knowing what to think.

Well, aren't you going to say something? asked One.

"Were you talking to me?" asked Clay.

Yes we're talking to you. This whole time we've been talking to you. Have you been listening?

The truth was Clay hadn't been sure to whom One or The Other had been talking.

Hello! yelled One.

"Yes. Sorry. I'm just trying to take it in."

Well, before you turn rock hard like me and my 'friend' over there, I recommend you go and check out the gallery.

"The gallery in the square?"

Good gracious! Yes! The only one!

It may not be a bad idea, conceded The Other. *At least then you can see the Potter's handiwork. He's really quite talented.*

Just remember, One inserted, *most of us turn out like Bricks. From the looks of you, even a brick may be a long shot.*

Talk about dreamkiller, said The Other.

Just telling it like it is, mocked One.

Excuse One, said The Other down to Clay, *he gets cranky when it rains. Water seeps in his cracks.*

A comment like that doesn't deserve a response. Look, Clay, whatever you do, promise me you won't let the Potter make you into a chamber pot.

Prayer for a Daughter

ONE AND THE Other were still bickering when Clay exited the alley. Their voices joined the rest that were jumbling around his mind. So far, the made things he had encountered seemed satisfied, for the most part, with their purposes, but there was something about each one that didn't seem satisfactory to Clay. He couldn't picture being a brick or a cup or a chamber pot. Then again, what if Clay's wants didn't matter? For all he knew, the Potter might take one look and send him to the dump. That was Sir Brownstone's prediction. What if they were right? They certainly believed they weren't wrong.

Clay's muddy feet sloshed along the cobblestones while he walked in the frustration of not knowing what he wanted to become. He sighed a long, dive bomb of a whistle. It waffled and fluttered through the confusion he was feeling inside.

Thank you, she said.

Startled, Clay looked up and gaped.

Behind a pane of glass stood a vase tall and slender. Her body rose from her square base, her corners twisting upward like dancing arms. Her translucent form shimmered with hues of orange, yellow and scarlet. It created the illusion of movement; it was like her very being was ablaze. As if by the passing through fire, she had become it. She was frozen in flame.

Clay had seen beautiful things before, but this truly was the most beautiful thing he had ever seen.

Were you looking for me? she asked.

Her voice was so smooth Clay almost melted.

Can you hear me through the windowpane? she asked.

Clay nodded slowly. The truth was he was only half-listening. Vase was so gorgeous it was like sight was the only sense that worked. Clay's forehead collided with the windowpane as if drawn by magnetic force. Embarrassed, he shot up like an exclamation point. He left a print. Desperately, he tried erasing the smudge, but the attempt only made it worse.

Vase giggled. It sounded like the twitter of early birds.

Are you Clay? she asked.

Clay lifted his arms as if to say 'Yes.'

I mean the Clay everyone is talking about?

"I'm being talked about?" he said with surprise.

Word gets around in a town this size.

"What are they saying?"

Oh, that you came from the hill country, that you risked your life to meet a teacup.

Clay's shoulder itched.

That you want to be made but are afraid to meet the Potter.

"I'm not afraid," said Clay, taken aback.

Then why haven't you gone to see him?

"I'm doing – research," he said awkwardly.

How is it coming? she kidded.

"Well, you know." Clay dragged his clumpy foot over the uneven ground. He was feeling a little out of his league.

It's all right to be afraid, Clay. Becoming isn't something one should enter into lightly.

Clay nodded as if he understood.

It's better to go through fire prepared.

Clay straightened. "You've been through fire?"

All clay passes through fire when it's made.

"Is it painful?" asked Clay, embarrassed to be asking such an ignorant question.

It is death, and there is pain in death. And like death, fire is final. Once you become there is no turning back. But also like death, there is life beyond it.

"Do you mean there is life after death?"

See for yourself, she said.

"I do," he said. "I mean, here you are."

Here I am, she said, *though I am nothing like I was before.*

"So the process is painful?"

To a degree, she answered. *First, you experience pressure; then, you torque and compress while your particles find the best ways to bond with each other. In the end you feel stronger than you have ever felt in your existence.*

"Is it uncomfortable to be so hard?"

No, she laughed. *Once you are made, you are complete. United. Whole. It's the best feeling in the world.*

"Are you ever restless?" he asked.

Never.

The way she said it, Clay believed her. "Do you have a name?" he asked.

Prayer for a Daughter.

"That's a name?"

She giggled. *It's the one the Potter gave me.*

"You are beautiful," said Clay clumsily.

I know, she said. There was no vanity in the way she said it.

"Did you ask the Potter to make you this way?"

The Potter does what he wants, she replied.

Clay had no doubt he had done his very best. "Can he make all clay look like you?"

I can't answer that, said Prayer for a Daughter. *I only know he doesn't.*

"There must have been something special about you to inspire him to make you this way," Clay said.

There is something special about all of us.

Clay pushed the response aside. "But you are unique. You are not like Brick or China. In all the world, I bet you are the only Prayer for a Daughter.

I imagine there are millions of prayers for daughters, many that are far more beautiful than me. I am only a sculpture.

These made things sure are frustrating, thought Clay. But then he remembered that Prayer for a Daughter could read thoughts, so he stopped thinking.

I know what you are trying to say, she continued. *Yes, it's true that I'm valuable, at least according to my price tag. And yes, the Potter made me this way on purpose. And yes, there are many things that I love about being unique and beautiful. But please understand, Clay, becoming made always comes with a cost.*

"Do you mean that the Potter will require me to pay?"

Not at all. What I mean is that we cannot have everything. My guess is that much of your fear has to do with this. You are afraid of what you will lose by becoming made. For you will lose something in the process. No one is completely self-satisfied.

"Are you saying that no made thing is happy?"

Happiness is a poor measure because happiness never lasts. What I'm saying is there are benefits and drawbacks to every purpose.

"What could you be missing?" asked Clay.

Nothing, Clay. Being a sculpture is very fulfilling. I wouldn't change a thing about who I am, but there are aspects about what I am that are not so wonderful. For instance, no one caresses me the way China is caressed. Because I'm fragile, the only fingers I feel are trembling ones. I'll tell you Clay, there are times I would trade all my beauty for a single loving touch. And though it's true I have a large price tag, no one will ever trust me with their life the way they trust their bricks. I'm no good when it comes to protection. So Clay, I ask you, what is more valuable, a person's possessions or a person's life? In that respect, I am worth less than Brick.

"You are not worth less than Brick. I could never believe that."

I don't believe it either. All the same, I'm not worth more. Don't you see? No purpose is more special than another. There are qualities about each one of us that give us significance. There are things about clay that are wonderful, too.

"But there are other things that are perfectly miserable."

You're right. But don't think becoming made is going to change that.

Clay sensed Prayer for a Daughter was more satisfied in being a sculpture than she was letting on. Maybe she was trying to lower his expectations so he wouldn't be disappointed when the Potter made him into a chamber pot.

"Thanks for the advice," Clay mumbled, hoping she hadn't read his last thought.

You're welcome, said Prayer for a Daughter before adding: *I said earlier that it was all right to be afraid. It is, Clay, but you should also know there is nothing to fear. If you want to be made there is no better place to go than to the Potter. He knows clay. I have every confidence that he will do his very best with you.*

"With what he has to work with," muttered Clay.

What was that?

"Nothing." Clay stretched. He had gotten stiff over the course of their conversation.

I hope I've been some help.

"You were," said Clay. The truth was he was confused.

Best of luck with the Potter.

At the name, a strange tingle tickled his neck behind the ears. It reminded Clay of something important. "Excuse me, Prayer for a Daughter?"

What is it, Clay?

"How do I find him?"

Prayer for a Daughter giggled.

"What's so funny?"

Oh nothing. It's just that I don't think you'll have any problem with that.

"Why?" asked Clay.

"Because I have found you," said the Potter.

Part Three —
The Potter

The Potter was about to do magic.

By the River

THE POTTER TOOK Clay by the elbow. His pace was not particularly fast, but there was purpose to it, which seemed to Clay a good sign since he was in the market for one.

"Where are we going?" Clay asked as they turned down a side street.

Deep wrinkles formed in the man's cheeks and around his eyes, but he gave no remark. The Potter was unremarkable in general. He was short but proportional with black hair, except for the gray tufts around his ears. His dirty fingernails were discolored and trimmed by happenstance, and his narrow nose was crooked like it had once been broken.

Besides these unremarkable attributes, and the fact that his clothes were filthy, the Potter had one characteristic worth noting.

His eyes looked like storm clouds. Cataracts made them that way. It was a condition that made eyesight about as difficult as
seeing *through* storm clouds – though Clay
didn't understand this at the time. The truth
is sight is always a matter of perspective.
And though it was true that the Potter did
not have normal-looking eyes, it certainly
appeared as if he knew where he was going.
At least he took a deep contented breath
when he stopped and said, "There's music in
the water, don't you think?"

Clay nodded nervously. Though it was
true Clay loved to listen to the music the
water made; unfortunately, all Clay could
think about at the moment was how, just yesterday, he had been mangled not so far from
here into a mess of stones, boot prints and
swords made from branches. Taking a breath,
the memory of Ned's rejection filled his lungs
like smoke. It sickened the stomach Clay
technically didn't have. "What are we doing
here?" he asked, forcing the question through
the lump in his throat.

"Ah yes, hear-ing," said the Potter as if
he was repeating Clay's last word. Sitting
down, the Potter leaned back on his arms

and *mmm*ed like he was savoring a slice of Mrs. Farmer's apple pie. "Hearing happens on either side of your head. Of course, when it's done right, hearing involves every atom of your being."

"But why are we here?" asked Clay, still confused.

But the only answer the Potter gave was a gentle tide of air coming through his nostrils. Clay waited for more of a response until the silence drew on so long it became deafening, and eventually Clay began to wonder if it wasn't him but the Potter who was waiting for the other to speak, which is what Clay finally did, figuring something was better than nothing. "I'm the kind of clay called brownstone, which, I'm told, is a pretty good clay to be," Clay began, feeling foolish, though it didn't stop him from continuing. "The Buena Vista Bell Tower is made of it. They came from a quarry called Hummelstown. I came from a deposit on Mule Lick Creek.

"The Bell Tower didn't think too highly of potters, but I met other made things who do: Brick, a teacup named China, Prayer for a Daughter of course. You saw me with her, so I don't need to be telling you," Clay paused mid-babble. "I guess what I'm trying to say is that I know I have all these twigs and stones sticking out here, there and everywhere; but if you help me get them out, I bet you can make something out of the rest of me."

The Potter seemed to nod; either that or he was falling asleep. It was hard to tell because his eyes were closed, and he was breathing heavily.

"There's this boy," said Clay, sensing no harm in continuing, "his name is Ned. He's my friend; at least, he was my friend. His father brought me to town as a surprise, but it didn't turn out the way we expected." Clay twisted inside.

The corners of the Potter's mouth quivered slightly.

"You should have seen the way Ned's face lit up when he saw the things you made. That's the reason I'm here. I was hoping you could make something of me. Something maybe a boy would like. What, I don't know. It's a hard decision. And important. I'll be living with the results for a very long time."

A small puff of air slipped between the Potter's lips. The puff was similar to the kind Clay made when he was thinking about big things. Under the circumstances, it made perfect sense, which is why Clay said: "So you see what I mean. That's why I didn't come to you right away. It was a crow's idea, actually. She advised me to talk with some made things first. You might think that a silly thing to do. Probably was. Talking with made things didn't help very much. Well, it did. Just not the way I hoped. The thing is I'm no closer to knowing what I want to become than when I started."

The Potter snored a little.

Clay blazed on: "Prayer for a Daughter said I was afraid. She's right. I am. Becoming made is a life changing experience. What if I become a mistake? Not that you make them. I've seen your handiwork. It's quite beautiful." Clay sighed. "It's just, as you can see, I'm a mess. But if you help me get these twigs and stones out, I'm sure you can make something wonderful out of the rest of me."

The Potter stirred a moment then let out a noise that sounded like a whinny.

"That's fine. I don't need to be wonderful. I'd be happy with anything," Clay thought a moment, "except a chamber pot. I promised Brick I wouldn't become one of those."

During Clay's speech, the sky had changed from blue to purple to ash. In the background, water jingled and swirled in the gray of dusk. The temperature dropped. The wind picked up.

Clay became keenly aware of how hard he was getting. "Excuse me, Mr. Potter?" he asked, trying to raise a finger. "I'm afraid I'm stuck."

The Potter didn't make a sound.

"This is not what I expected," Clay whispered because his lips were freezing shut. He tried to move. He strained, strained, until suddenly his arm broke off! Frantically, he tried to stretch his legs, but they also threatened to detach. Clay was paralyzed, a statue that could only see and hear – which got him nowhere.

It was dark when the Potter finally patted Clay on the head. "Stay here," he said. Clay did, of course. He couldn't do otherwise.

The Potter placed a dark hand on Clay's cheek. He walked away.

Clay tried to call after him, to tell him *Stop. Come back.* But his slice of a mouth was locked shut. Anyway, what was the point? The Potter was gone. Night had come. And Clay was left in the dark. He listened to the river tinkle and chime.

It ran as if to mock him.

Dust to Dust

ALL NIGHT, CLAY agonized over what he had done to deserve this. Was it something he said? Was it some kind of punishment? A form of rejection? Or had he simply been forgotten?

Clay had no answers, and the questions only filled the time.

They drained him.

A week crept past, and by the end of it, Clay's patience had run its course. He wanted to leave – if only he could get his legs to move – but he couldn't get his legs to move. And there was no sign of the Potter.

His absence was like a cloudy sky, and the only conclusion Clay could draw from it was that he'd been lied to. Brick, China and Prayer for a Daughter all told him the Potter could be trusted. Of course they did. They had potential: Brick was strong, China was helpful, and Prayer for a Daughter was one of a kind. Clay was different. Clay was a mess.

This was where trust got him.

If the man was a magician, he was all trick. And this particular disappearing act wasn't funny.

One by one, his appendages detached. His neck severed. His head teetered when the breeze picked up. Condensation seeped into his broken places and froze; in the morning, the ice melted and left cracks. It was only a matter of time before he crumbled to pieces.

Clay lost his head. It rolled a few feet then stopped.

In three weeks, he had been reduced to a block around a broken heart, which he technically didn't have. Reality was setting in: Here, alone, Clay was going to erode until there was nothing left. Birds would peck through his remains for worms. People would tread on him never knowing he existed. It was little consolation, but Sir Brownstone's prediction was wrong. Clay wasn't going to end up in the dump. Clay was going to vanish in the dirt.

It made what Ned did feel like child's play.

And as days amounted to weeks, Clay even lost that – the orchard, the deposit, the boy – they were no longer real, just shadows and sketches. Motion was the dream. In fact, as Clay slipped in and out of consciousness, he sometimes felt himself running and twisting and bending and twirling, swinging his friend in the valley of a *U*...and in those moments Clay could almost remember the sensation, but then he'd wake to realize it was only his imagination. Life was illusion.

And the Potter was a phantom. He haunted Clay. The man's invisible presence was like a penetrating force, a dark cloud. Every once in awhile, a chill would shroud Clay's body like a sheet, as if someone was standing there, watching, but then the sensation would pass, and eventually Clay became numb to even that...

...which is perhaps why the explosion felt so jarring...

Clean

THIS IS THE end, Clay cried as the sledge-hammer reduced his pieces to rubble. The hammer slammed. It smashed his rubble to marbles; then crushed his marbles to granules, his granules to dust.

The straws of the broom sifted through his remains like a forest of knives. They swept him onto a sheet that was carried to a barrel then dumped. The walls echoed. Suddenly, a torrent of water crashed on top of him. Splishing and sploshing, a blunt paddle stirred Clay into liquid. Twigs and leaves bobbed to the surface; stones trickled to the bottom of the barrel. Clay floated in what amounted to be himself – a strange experience to say the least. However, he had no chance to absorb it because the next instant he was being lifted and poured into another barrel. Then another.

And another. It was happening so fast Clay failed to realize that the stones and twigs and leaves weren't coming with him. A sieve was catching them. And *he* was filtering through. All Clay sensed was that he was experiencing something that could only be described as strangely comfortable, comfortably odd.

Like being reborn into what he always had been.

It's ironic, but the word that comes to mind is *clean.*

When it was over, the Potter carried the barrel of muddy water to a shelf. Every couple days, as Clay settled to the bottom, the Potter drained water off the top.

And just like that, though it took some time, Clay became clay again. It was a slow discovery, though no less incredible, for it produced in Clay a glimmer of what actually had happened. The hardness, the crushing, the liquifying – the Potter wasn't punishing him; he was *preparing* him. For what Clay didn't know. But it stood to reason that the Potter wouldn't have put Clay through it all if there wasn't one, a reason that is.

And another thing: Clay discovered *he could hear!* The chattery clapping of dead leaves in the wind, the *krishshssh krishshssh* sliding of the Potter's feet, the man's clear-as-the-blue-sky whistle – it reminded Clay of what the Potter said to him by the river – that hearing done right involved every atom of your being. The Potter was right. Clay *heard.* Sight was coming in the same way. And as for smell, Clay couldn't avoid it. He reeked. He was like wet barnyard and swamp cabbage mixed with a dash of horseradish and stale cucumber. It was enough to make you gag.

Although when the Potter came near, he breathed in Clay's odor like he was breathing in the flowers.

Curiosity Takes Over

A FEW DAYS later, Clay awoke to the familiar *krishshssh krishshssh* shuffle of the Potter's feet.

"Good morning," said the Potter.

Good morning, she replied.

Who was there? Who was talking? Clay wondered.

The Potter's knees cracked. He must have squatted. Clay heard crinkling paper.

"Are you ready?" asked the Potter.

Ready for what? Clay wondered. Curiosity was getting the best of him.

I think so, she said. *I'm a little nervous.*

Suddenly, Clay realized what was happening: *Clay like him was about to be made.* It was too much to sit by. He simply had to witness the transformation.

The Potter was about to do magic.

So gathering himself, Clay jumped from the barrel to the ground and quickly formed into something boy-sized and human-like. And for the first time, he took in the world that was the Potter's house.

It was a mess. Chaos was more like it. Strange instruments sprouted out of pots like bouquets of flowers without the flowers. Pottery in various stages of made-ness was scattered like puzzle pieces. Buckets, sheets and what amounted to junk were stacked underneath tables or stashed on shelves or strewn on the floor. There wasn't a direct line to anything. At the same time, there seemed to be an order to the clutter, as if the room was actually an elaborate maze.

Clay blended into it as best he could. From behind an empty barrel, he watched the Potter wind his way to a table. A grayish-bluish ball sat in his hand. He tossed her in the air and caught her. Clay crept toward them, all the while spying as the Potter lifted her slightly then slammed her against the tabletop.

The room rattled. The table jumped. Clay squeezed his eyes, wincing at the force, but curiosity quickly pried them back open.

The Potter peeled back the flattened clay. His hands were pale, ghostly. The sinews in his forearms flexed. He smashed the clay a second time. Again the earth quaked. Again Clay flinched.

What was he doing?

"Wedging," said the Potter. His dark hair swayed like branches. His eyes tensed like a thunderstorm. His jaw set. "Wedging clears you of air pockets," he continued, beginning to knead. "It aligns you down to the particle," talking through the thrust. "Makes you resilient," grunting now in rhythm. The Potter's muscular arms drove down like lightning bolts. They came taut with each transfer of weight. "Things work best when their atoms work together."

The gray-blue clay rocked back and forth as if she understood.

Clay could tell she was relaxing, becoming malleable.

Sweat pooled along the Potter's brow. He brooded like a bird over her nest. Air burst through his nostrils like a bull. It was like the Potter was transferring his energy into the clay, for it looked like she was moving by herself. Grooves appeared along her surface like the overlapping petals of a flower. Like a cupped hand, she had become an extension of the Potter's. They moved in rhythm like dancers.

As a matter of fact, the longer Clay observed their interaction, the less violent and the more graceful it appeared. Even the beginning, but certainly now – it was *intimate* – so personal that, for a moment, Clay averted his eyes. Not for long, however, because the beauty of it was irresistible. It was beautiful like Prayer for a Daughter. It was beautiful like a prayer.

Like love.

With great subtlety, the Potter altered the steps to the dance. The clay in his hands folded gracefully into a ball though nothing like the ball she had been. She was gleaming. The Potter lifted her in his palm. He studied her, or was he admiring her? He was looking *through* her not *at* her – his eyes so intense Clay found himself lost in them – in the wonder of what it was like to receive a look like that.

But the dance wasn't over.

The Wheel

THE POTTER ESCORTED her through the maze to a platform he called *the wheel*. It was a round disk about waist high that was attached to a larger disk just off the floor. The way they were connected, if the Potter spun one, the other would spin as well.

Clay maneuvered closer.

"Is this where I'll be made?" she asked. Clay heard apprehension in her voice.

"No, Clayre," answered the Potter, sitting at a bench.

Did the Potter just call the clay, Clayre?

He touched her with assurance. "Don't be afraid. You are well on your way." He picked up a teapot. Steam wafted from the spout. Tilting it, he poured some water into a bowl then pressed a spoonful of tea leaves into a steeper, which he placed inside the pot.

"What does the water do?" asked Clayre.

"In two minutes it will magically transform into tea," he answered, waving his hand.

"No, the water in the bowl," she said, giggling.

"Let me show you," the Potter said, answering with a swift kick that spun the wheel to life and sent Clayre spinning like a renegade carousel horse. The Potter pumped his leg until he was satisfied with the wheel's rotation. Then placing his hands on Clayre, he *pat, pat* patted her into a pointy mound. She spun out of control. He dipped his hands in the water. He hunched over the swirling clay, curving his wet fingers around her as if he was warming them by a fire.

"First, we center," he said.

Clay wondered if Clayre knew what centering was. He had a feeling they were both about to find out.

The Potter leaned in; and starting from her base, he pressed his hands together. Finger-grooves corkscrewed as she rose, his hands guiding, rising, spiraling upward until they joined together like he was praying with them. Clayre looked like a trumpet standing on end.

"Cone up," the Potter said.

Now the Potter mentioned it, she did resemble a cone.

He scraped some-of-Clayre off his fingers and re-wet his hands. "Down to center," he said, pushing the cone with the web between his thumbs and fingers, shaping her into what resembled an overturned bowl. She was so symmetrical she looked motionless even though she was spinning.

The Potter hovered over her. His eyes were boiling thunderclouds – energy and impulse – looking *through* her once again. "Here we go," he said. "Hole in. Draw out the sides. Compress the bottom. Pull." He performed each action as he said it. Then, with only a thumb and finger to guide, Clayre rose into a cylinder like magic. *Right before their eyes.*

"Ah!" Clay exclaimed, unable to contain himself.

But if the Potter heard Clay's outcry, he ignored it. He worked as if transfixed: massaging Clayre's surface, drawing her up, smoothing her inside and out. His hands never departed from her, nor did they part from each other. Together, tenderly, they moved – the very hands that had punched and pounded – it was hard to believe they could be this gentle.

The Potter's eyes arced like rainbows as he wet his hands and went back to work. No, work was not the word for it. The Potter was having too much fun for this to be work.

He whistled even.

And Clay looked on as the Potter flattened his hands and transformed Clayre-the-cylinder into Clayre-the-beautiful-basin.

Clay gasped again.

The Potter paid no notice. He was concentrating on the one he was shaping. "Wonderful," he beamed, the wheel slowing to a stop. With a string, the Potter separated the basin from it. Carefully, he placed her on the bench beside him. He wiped his dirty hands down his pant legs, then took a sip of tea.

Time to get moving, thought Clay, unsure how the Potter would react at Clay's espionage. He didn't want to chance it. Still, moving wasn't easy. *Clay like him had just been made. One day, what happened to Clayre would happen to him.* It made him lightheaded to think about it. He was full to the point of dizziness. He knees were wobbly, his head was spinning and the maze of the room was disorienting when a voice froze him in his tracks.

"Leaving so soon?"

The Kiln

"DON'T WORRY, CLAY. If I didn't want you to see, I wouldn't have let you watch," the Potter said, placing the teacup to the side.

"You knew I was watching?" asked Clay both shocked and unsettled.

"I know clay," said the Potter through a sly smile. He motioned to him, "This way."

Clay shuddered. The last time the Potter had said those words he had left Clay by the river. "Where are we going?" he asked warily.

"The kiln," said the Potter, *krrsssshhh krrssshhhing* to the door.

"What's a kiln?" asked Clay, following despite his nerves.

"It's an oven."

"Are you cooking something?"

"Not that kind of oven. A kiln is where clay is made."

Made? Clay thought what he had just witnessed was clay being made.

"The wheel is where I give clay form, but clay is not made until it's fired," the Potter explained.

Clay cried: "But you haven't formed me yet!"

The Potter laughed. "You're right, my friend. You are in no shape to be fired."

"Oh," said Clay, wishing he had not opened his mouth.

"I need to check on some plates. Would you mind keeping me company?"

"Yes," said Clay – or was the proper answer *no*?

"Good," said the Potter.

"I do like fresh air," Clay admitted.

"Me, too," said the Potter, leading them outside. "The wisteria is in bloom. Would you like me to pinch you a bigger nose?"

"Sure," said Clay. "Thanks."

"My pleasure," he said, completing the touches as Clay wondered why the Potter was going through the trouble. Clay didn't need a nose to smell, and the Potter knew it. However, the reason would have to remain a mystery because they had arrived at what appeared to be a tiny house.

The squarish structure was taller than Clay, shorter than the Potter, but wider than the two of them put together. Made of stone, a narrow chimney rose out its top, and a small opening yawned out its front. Tips of grass were charred along its base.

This was the kiln. The sight of it filled Clay with foreboding.

He was standing at death's door.

"It takes a lot of heat to make clay," explained the Potter, testing the stone for temperature with his hand.

"How much?" asked Clay.

"As much as two thousand degrees," said the Potter. "A human would die at half that temperature."

"Does clay die at two thousand degrees?"

"Yes," said the Potter very matter of fact. Without further explanation, he fell to hands and knees then crawled through the opening so deep Clay could only see the soles of his shoes. They were holey.

Clay heard *clinking*. A minute later the Potter scuttled backward with a stack of plates in his hands. A pile of shards lay on top.

"The new rector requested these to commemorate the church's recent growth in attendance." The Potter took one from the stack. The plate was the color of Mule Lick Creek after a rain. In the center was a smooth carving of a white oak leaves with acorns. Around the border was a nest of squiggles. "This is called inlay," he explained, touching the pattern. "I used the leaves from the oak tree behind the rectory as my model."

"What is this along the edge?" asked Clay, pointing at the border.

"Inlay as well," said the Potter from his knees.

"But what is it supposed to be?" asked Clay.

"Roots," said the Potter. "No fruit without roots. I chose an oak tree because the best growth is slow growth, and the best fruit is for others not ourselves."

"Do you think the rector," Clay didn't know what a rector was, "will understand the meaning?"

"No," said the Potter simply.

His answer bothered Clay.

"They're good, aren't they?" said the Potter.

"I think they're too good for somebody who will not understand them," Clay said, surprising himself with his honesty.

"They'll find their voice presently," said the Potter. He lifted the plate eye-level.

"But they will only be plates!" shouted Clay.

"No, Clay. They are far more than plates."

"But the rector won't understand the meaning." The thought was making Clay very upset.

In the meantime, the Potter turned his attention to the broken plate. He tossed the pieces into a bucket of shards.

Clay hadn't seen the bucket until that moment. "Now what are you doing?" he cried.

"What do you think I'm doing?"

"You're tossing those pieces in a bucket."

"They're broken," said the Potter.

"What?" cried Clay.

"Plates break sometimes."

"That's it? After all that clay went through to become made?"

"There is no more clay. The clay is no more."

"But that clay went into the fire to become a plate."

"Yes," said the Potter, "things do not always turn out the way we mean them to."

Clay could hardly believe what his ears were hearing.

"Not all was lost," said the Potter.

"Easy for you to say. This clay lost its life!"

The Potter made no reply.

"Doesn't that make you sad?" It made Clay terribly sad.

But the Potter's eyes were unreadable clouds.

Dawne

"COME, CLAY, WE have another errand to run," said the Potter.

But Clay didn't move. He was shaken, stunned at the sudden uncertainty of life.

In the end, the Potter was forced to carry Clay on his shoulders like a child. He took hold of the bucket of broken pieces. The shards *chinkled* as they lifted from the ground.

"You forgot your plates," whispered Clay, his voice still shaky.

"It's good to allow things to cool. It prevents division."

"Oh," Clay said, realizing that a bucket of rejects was his only traveling companion. "We're going to the dump, aren't we?" Clay swallowed.

The Potter whistled a few bars then said, "The dump is an extraordinary place.

You wouldn't believe the wonderful things people throw away. Just last week, I found these shoes."

That explains the holes, thought Clay. Extraordinary or not, he had no interest in being dumped. At the moment, the only thing interesting Clay was escape. But just when Clay was about to leap to a branch, the Potter said: "Alas, we don't have time to go to the dump today. Perhaps tomorrow."

"Oh," said Clay, remaining where he was. "So where –?"

"Watch your head," interrupted the Potter. "Why?"

"I believe willow branches are about to knock you off your perch."

"Whoa!" Clay cried as one nearly did.

"Don't say I didn't warn you," laughed the Potter, his shoulders bobbing through the tendril-like branches. Clay clung to his collar.

"Who's there!" came a voice midway between a shriek and a bark. "You sneaking up on me again?"

"Not very well, it seems," replied the Potter to the woman now in view.

She was wide and earthy with braids that came down like the willow branches Clay just survived. Her rosy cheeks resembled Ned's sister. Her clothes, on the other hand, resembled Betsy's rag dolls.

"This is Dawne," said the Potter.

"Who'd you think it was?" she said. "Oh, you're talking to him." She flapped her hand in a wave. "Hey, little fella. Enjoy the ride?"

Clay opened the slice of his mouth, but nothing came out.

"What's that? Cat got your tongue? Looks like he's caught that silent disease of yours."

"It's not a disease, Dawne."

"It sure as heck drives the rest of us crazy," she chided, turning her attention to Clay. "He didn't tell you where you were coming, did he?"

Clay shook his head.

"You really should stop leaving folks in the dark. We don't like it."

The Potter didn't answer.

"Of course. You have nothing to say for yourself." She made a motion to the bucket. Without invitation, she began sifting with an index finger. "You got reds this time? I need some reds." Picking up a shard, she felt it with her thumb. Her lips parted. Her crooked teeth were caked in yellow. "What you want for them?" she asked.

"Same price as always."

"I earn more now. I can pay you what they're worth." She rubbed her fingers together.

"We agreed on the price a long time ago," he said.

"A long time ago, you gave me pieces for free," she smiled.

"Because you couldn't pay," he replied.

"But then I could. And I did. Don't you forget it. Now, I can pay more."

"What does more get you?" asked the Potter.

"It gets me what's cooking," she said, pointing back to the smoke coming from her chimney. "You want some?"

Clay rose as the Potter filled his lungs. "Well, seeing as you mentioned it –"

"Just like you," she said, pointing a finger, "showing up when something's cooking."

A blush came to the Potter's dirty cheeks. "Has it happened before? I hadn't noticed," he said, feigning innocence.

Dawne slapped her thigh before placing the hand on her hip. "Can't fool me, Potter." Her laugh sounded like a cough.

"Nor would I want to," he said. "But first, would you mind showing us your progress?"

"Certainly," she said, smiling her dirty teeth. Her eyes, on the contrary, were as sparkling clean as a new day. "What's your name, little fella?" she asked, reaching out a hand.

"Clay," he said, dropping to the ground.

"Creative," she replied through a rusty laugh. "Come along then, Clay. Let's see what we can see."

Clay took her hand. It was dirty but delicate and would have been elegant had her life been different. But as it is for all of us, life had been what it had been. She seemed content, though, and possessed a vibrant step – like her knees were fortified with springs.

"This is my studio. Better than that musty room the Potter's got."

"Are you a potter, too?" Clay asked.

She laughed. "Too muddy for my liking though I do work with ceramics from time to time. See," she said, pointing to a table covered in multi-colored fragments.

"It's –" started Clay.

"Not finished, I know. I've been waiting (for ages!) for Potter to show up with reds." Her finger drew Clay's attention to the brilliant whatever-it-was on the table. "It's called a mosaic. A picture made from hundreds of tiny pieces. The town council commissioned it. They wanted something that would reflect our agricultural heritage. Now, how am I supposed to do that without reds? We're the apple basket of the heartland for heaven's sake!"

"I'm truly sorry," apologized the Potter.

Judging by the slice of her smile, Clay sensed Dawne wasn't as upset as she was letting on. Placing the bucket on the table, she placed Clay on the top of her head. "You can hold the braids," she said. "Don't worry. You can't make my hair any more ratty than it is."

Clay held on. He liked Dawne even if she was a little rough around the edges.

The mosaic looked entirely different from this new perspective. From the ground, it looked like a random scattering of fragments. Here, a picture emerged. There was the town, the square, the bell tower, places beyond it. Places he had never seen. An expanse of blue along the top. Was it water? Sky? He was about to ask when Dawne said, "Shush, I need to concentrate." Her hands went through the contents of the bucket like she was going through the mail. "Nice inlay," she said, admiring one of the shards from the rector's broken plate. "What is that? Roots? Are there more?"

Clay followed her fingers as she placed a flake from the plate that had been broken. The fingers had gone upstream, to a creek in the hill country, to an orchard of trees that were missing apples, needing reds. Needing fragments – like brown pieces with roots. And as Clay watched Dawne put the tiny shard in place, a light dawned inside of him. *All was not lost.* The plate, the broken one that had lost a purpose, had gained another one here – a purpose, perhaps, even more meaningful. Even if it was attained through brokenness.

They shared a meal (the Potter filling his bowl three times), and now they were standing by the willow tree, saying good-bye. Dawne patted Clay on the head. "Don't let Potter get to you," she said with a wink. "He means well."

"Thanks for showing me your mosaic," said Clay, smiling up at her.

"The pleasure's all mine. Which reminds me, don't you dare let that man leave without getting paid."

"You paid me plenty already," laughed the Potter, patting his belly.

"No you don't!" she said. "I swear he does this every time. Wait here. Clay, don't let that man leave." Turning, she gathered her rag doll skirt in her hands.

But there was nothing Clay could do. The moment she turned so did they.

An orchard of trees that were missing apples, needing reds.

Routine
and Restlessness

FROM THAT DAY forward, Clay kept the Potter company. It began each morning when the Potter shuffled into the studio from the adjoining room where he slept. Clay slept on a wooden platform underneath cheesecloth (which is made of cotton, not cheese), and the day would begin when the Potter peeled the cheesecloth back and gave Clay a slap.

"Hey!" Clay would say, no longer needing a mouth to say it. "There are gentler ways to wake somebody, you know."

"None more effective," replied the Potter with a smile. In all honesty, the slap was on the mild side. Mornings made Clay stiff, and the stiffness made him grouchy. "Mind if I get you in shape?" the Potter would ask. "*Grrr*," Clay would grumble while the Potter formed him into something that looked very much like a boy.

It brought to mind those mornings Clay would shape himself into something boy-sized and human-like for Ned. Clay often found himself wondering about him… Had his family returned to the orchard? Had Ned returned to the creek? Did he play with another clay like him? Or had Ned's interests changed to made things? Had his imagination been relegated to what he read in books? Or was his belief gone all together? Mostly, Clay wondered, was he happy?

For the time being, Clay was content. After all he had been through, the simple act of being shaped in the morning felt like enough, at least for the time being.

He still longed to be made. Each night, from his spot underneath the cheesecloth, he wondered about it – what it was like, how it felt, what he'd become. He imagined being made into something so wonderful it would make a boy like Ned smile forever. How great that would be! The thought comforted him as he slipped each night into sleep. For each day that passed brought him one day closer to the day he would be made.

The Potter never let on when that day would be. Based on his actions, the man wasn't in a hurry. He seemed satisfied simply with the routine. No, *routine* wasn't quite the word for it because once the Potter finished shaping Clay, there was no telling what the day would bring.

Some days were spent by the wheel. There, Clay accompanied the Potter while the Potter formed other clays into vases, cups and plates. Lately, they had been on a candlestick kick. Nothing but candlesticks for three straight days. On other days, the Potter trimmed pieces he had formed already. Using hooks and knives, he'd whittle objects into their final shape. Strings of excess clay would curl away like worms and fall from the wheel to the floor like wood shavings. What remained on the wheel was placed on a shelf where it stayed until it was *knock hard*. Only then was it ready to be fired. That happened at the kiln. Clay kept his distance there, though he was always eager to see how the objects came out.

Clay learned it took multiple firings before an object was complete. The first time through was called *biscuit firing* (which meant the pieces were hard and grainy, not edible). Afterward, the Potter would color the piece with glaze, which once dried, would be fired again. Only then did the clay become made.

In other words, becoming made was a process.

Clay witnessed every step, even the ones that didn't feel like steps at all. Like the days the Potter took Clay *prospecting*, which was basically just taking a walk. Or the days they sat by the river for *inspiration*, which was exactly like daydreaming. Most days, Clay didn't feel like he was accomplishing much of anything. Apart from the company he kept, Clay never felt like he had much to offer. He spent a lot of time wondering when it would be his turn.

The Potter never gave the slightest inclination.

Spring turned to summer. Summer was turning to fall.

And Clay remained clay.

Don't get the wrong impression. Clay enjoyed keeping the Potter company. He liked it very much, and the Potter liked it, too. The man demonstrated it in a number of ways – like the minutes he spent on Clay's earlobe. Both of them knew Clay didn't need ears to hear, and yet, there was the Potter wasting time, shaping each one like a flying buttress. Then there was the way he sat next to Clay while they listened to the music in the water. And how the Potter told him stories before tucking him snug underneath his cheesecloth every night. And how every morning the Potter's cloudy eyes arced like rainbows at the sight of him. And how they spent the days together. Clay accompanied the Potter wherever he went, and on the way they would talk about all sorts of things – like how trees grew or what caused the colors in a rainbow. Clay could ask the Potter anything, and the Potter did the same. He was interested in Clay's opinion. He even acted them. The truth was Clay had not been this loved in all his existence.

There was just one problem: nothing happened.

That's not true. Things happened. The problem was nothing happened to Clay. And worse: as the days, weeks, and months went by, Clay began to worry that the Potter didn't have any intention to do anything about it.

He became restless.

Things about the Potter became irritating, like how he shuffled – *krishshssh, krishshssh* – what an annoying sound! The man never lifted his feet! Or washed! Of course Clay didn't wash either but that was beside the point. The Potter was filthy. He wore the same dirty clothes every day. Plus, though the Potter never pointed out the fact, it was obvious that his whistle was far superior to Clay's. It made Clay never want to whistle again. But even that wasn't the worst thing – the worst thing about the Potter was how he never brought up the subject of being made. Of all the things Clay couldn't stand about the Potter, his silence was the worst.

Death and Departure

SEPTEMBER THAT YEAR was abnormally warm. The Potter called it Indian Summer. Clay called it misery. That he was restless and irritated didn't help, not to mention the fact that the Potter acted as if he didn't have a care in the world.

That morning, they had been meandering by the river for reasons only the Potter knew. Clay trudged beside him. It wasn't difficult; they were hardly moving. The difficulty was the Potter because for the last ten minutes, he had been going on and on about the injustice done to dandelions for being classified a weed instead of a flower. Finally, Clay decided he had suffered enough. "What about me?" he said, stopping in his tracks.

The Potter stopped, too. The sun seemed hotter than it felt just seconds before. "What about you?" he asked.

"I want to know about fire," answered Clay.

"It's hot," replied the Potter.

"I'm serious," said Clay.

"You're right. I'm sorry," he apologized. "What do you want to know?"

"Is it dangerous?" Clay asked.

"Yes," said the Potter, "if your current life is important to you."

"So is death bad?"

"Death happens."

"What do you mean?"

"We all die, Clay," said the Potter.

"Why can't you just say what you mean?" pleaded Clay. He was getting angry. He didn't entirely know why.

The Potter came down to Clay's level. Summer sweat beaded along his brow. He put a hand on Clay's shoulder. "Ask me what you really want to ask."

Clay didn't have the foggiest idea what he wanted to ask, except that he started talking: "I just don't get it. All I do is sit around while over and over you give purposes to everything else."

"Yes," said the Potter.

"It's like you don't even see me." If Clay had the capacity for tears, they would have been muddying his face.

"What are you asking?" asked the Potter. His cloudy eyes looked through Clay the way his cloudy eyes did.

"When will it be my turn?" Clay shouted.

"Your turn for what?" The Potter let his hand drop from Clay's shoulder.

"To be made!" Clay stomped for emphasis.

"You are Clay."

"I don't want to be Clay. I want to be something else. Some thing, don't you see? To have meaning like the others. A purpose or a reason. Why won't you give me one?"

"I haven't."

Clay couldn't tell if the Potter was answering a question or asking one. He was so furious it was difficult to understand anything. "What's wrong with me?" he yelled.

"Nothing is wrong with you, Clay."

"Then why don't you treat me the way you treat the others?"

"I do what I want to do," replied the Potter simply.

"What does that mean?" asked Clay astonished.

The Potter reached out to Clay, but Clay pushed his hand away.

"Don't touch me!"

"Clay," said the Potter.

"Don't call me that! I don't want to be Clay. I want to be Bowl or Cup or Prayer for a Daughter. I want a name like that. I've been waiting all this time to get a name like that." Clay was shaking. "I can't believe that after all you've put me through, you refuse to have the decency to give me one."

"What do you want to become?" asked the Potter.

"I don't care! You're the Potter."

"Well, if it's up to me, I want you to be Clay."

Clay couldn't believe what he heard. "Haven't you listened to a word I said?" he cried.

The Potter said nothing.

Clay stood there, motionless, stuck; while inside it was as if something finally broke. Anger flamed in his gut. Disappointment churned his heart into a hurricane. Hope was gone. The Potter had taken it. He had left Clay empty-handed.

Words roared out of him in a torrent. "So that's how it is. Don't worry. I read your silence loud and clear. You think I'm good for nothing." Clay's intricately carved eyes fell downcast. "I'm worthless. You just don't have the courage to tell me."

The Potter remained silent.

"I can't believe it's taken me this long to figure it out."

The Potter's eyes had never been cloudier.

Clay stared straight into them. "I thought you loved me."

The Potter's eyes grew dark.

"You never loved me."

The Potter didn't say a word.

"Well, if nothing is all you have to say, I'm leaving."

The Potter stayed quiet.

"Stop me if you want."

The Potter stood there.

"Say something!" Clay screamed.

The Potter said nothing.

"I hate you," said Clay.

The Potter didn't move.

Clay uttered a cry. It was loud and horrible and unearthly and came from the deepest fabric of his being. It was the voice of despair, of shattered hope and the emptiness of silence. It was the last thing he said before he turned and ran away.

The Potter did not go after him.

Part Four —
What Happened

The two scurried to a nook behind the stairwell.

Lost

THE NEXT THREE hours were a blind frenzy of fields and forests and country cottages and barking dogs and crunching leaves and buzzing insects until finally Clay collapsed in a meadow surrounded by trees. He was lost.

He was lost in more ways than one.

The fallow ground was uneven beneath his feet. It seemed to be forgotten, nameless, a nothing-special-kind-of-place – a perfect spot for a worthless lump of dirt to crumble to pieces and never be heard from again.

End of story.

Once upon a time, there was a lump of Clay who thought he could become something. Nothing happened. The end. That was it. His existence had been for nothing. In the end, that was all he was good for. So in the middle of the nameless meadow, Clay hunched into a mound and waited for the end to happen.

Afternoon turned to evening.

The sun set.

The temperature cooled.

The stars came out.

The moon rose.

Day broke.

The sun rose.

The day grew hot.

Crows cackled.

Clay gave them a cold shoulder.

The sun set.

The stars sparkled from their spots in the universe.

Clay didn't care for their company.

A stray dog sniffed him.

Clay punched him in the nose.

The next day, flies landed on his head.

Clay didn't shoo them away.

He was getting hard.

Depressed.

Cracks emerged. He was breaking apart.

The sun set.

The experience reminded him of when the Potter left him by the river. Although this time, it was Clay that had left; and this time,

Clay didn't care. *At least at the end I'll become something*, he thought: *dirt.* It was little comfort for a life with no purpose.

Clay's back looked like a turtle shell. Between his hunch and the cracks he could have been one – a turtle, playing hide-and-seek by himself. It was a cruel metaphor because now he was feeling the dagger pain of memory – of Ned and the games they played that summer the boy believed in him….

The door creaked as they slipped inside.

The farmhouse had always been off limits, but Ned wanted to show Clay his room. It was upstairs, and they were tiptoeing toward it when they heard Mother's foot against the porch steps outside.

"A Monster! This way!" whispered Ned, taking Clay by the hand. "To my secret place. We're safe from Monster's there." The two scurried to a nook behind the stairwell. They hunched in the shadows, a hole in the wood staring up at them like a quizzical eyeball. Ned and Clay held their breaths while the Monster, otherwise known as Mother, walked by without the slightest diversion to her direction. The kitchen door closed behind her, and Ned and Clay ran out the front safe and sound.

...Clay never made it to Ned's room. The house, the orchard, his friend – he would never see them again. If only he could. If only he was given the chance to tell Ned he was forgiven. That what happened by the river was a mistake. Child's play. Even if it wasn't, Clay forgave him. He loved Ned. How he wished they could be together again – even if the boy no longer believed. Even if time was like a river with no way to defy the current.

What happened by the river. Clay couldn't escape the memory. The Potter's cloudy eyes... his unreadable silence... his outstretched hand, and Clay had pushed his hand away. Their conversation came back to him in a flood. All the words Clay said. He regretted many of them. Not the ones about being made, but the anger that was there. He'd take it back if he could.

But it was too late.

Flies arrived.

Flies departed.

Clay had gone too far downstream. The old life was too far away.

He could no longer move. Soon he would be no longer.

Night had come.

And Clay plunged into a sleep most uncomfortable. It felt like death by rodeo – like some supernatural force had lassoed, tethered and dragged his body through fields and forests and country cottages and barking dogs and crunching leaves and buzzing insects then replanted it by force. He heard groaning, the tolling of a bell. It was so clear Clay could hardly believe he dreamt it.

He hadn't. Suddenly, Clay realized, what had happened was something real. Only, the reality was a nightmare. It was raining. Water covered his body like a death shroud. Drips of doom seeped down his cracks. Fate sunk in. The end was near. It was only a matter of time before he disintegrated into oblivion. And Clay had no way to stop it while it seemed as if the rain had changed to hail, for it was thundering all around him. It pummeled him like fists.

Then sunshine. Warmth. From the fissures in his back, steam was rising like tiny vapor prayers to heaven. But it was still raining? Water trickled down his sodden cheek. And yet, sunlight shined there, too. Clay pried his eyes open, but his sight was fuzzy. Sounds were garbled. The thunder was relentless.

Though slowly, he realized he was not dying. He was softening. Mobility was returning.

He was Clay again.

It wasn't raining at all. Suddenly, Clay realized, it had never been raining.

The Potter had come.

Sunset

"WHERE AM I?" Clay asked.

Deep wrinkles formed in the Potter's cheeks and around his eyes as he placed one hand on Clay's head, and the other on the center of Clay's chest. "Hear," he said.

Clay listened to the river's gurgles, swirls and trickles as they danced through every atom of his being. "How did I get here?" he asked.

"Effort," answered the Potter warmly. "Now, hold still," he said, using his thumbs to smooth Clay's face. It was like he was wiping tears away. And Clay watched closely as the Potter sliced a mouth, drew a lip, pinched a nose, curled an ear, twisted hair, and pulled an earlobe. He even placed a dimple in Clay's chin, just like the one in his. And when he was done, he cupped Clay's face in his hands. There was no looking away.

Until finally, the Potter turned his attention to Clay's shoulders. His hair swayed like the willows. It was then Clay noticed the deep scratches on the Potter's neck. The clotted blood on his ear. The missing button on his shirt. The rip in his denim pants. The gash on his right leg. The Potter was filthy, a complete mess – because of him – the Potter had become that way *for Clay*. After all Clay had said to him, after what Clay had done...here was the Potter kneeling at his feet, molding and shaping them like they were the feet of a prince.

The Potter limped to the river's edge to wash his hands and face. He limped back.

Clay saw the fatigue in his shoulders, the pain in his step. And as Clay watched him struggle, he yearned to call to him. But words like *thank you* and *I'm sorry* didn't possess the weight of gratitude he felt at the moment – the great appreciation that surged through every mineral and molecule of his being like an electrical pulse – the love Clay felt for this man who had storm clouds for eyes, this Potter who had searched through fields and forests and barking dogs and buzzing insects, this friend who had gone after him after he had run away.

There was odd symmetry to it all, for they had been *here* before: the first time to be broken, the second to be put back together. The Potter had done both.

He was using his hands to find a seat.

"You can't see," said Clay, realizing now what he probably should have noticed long ago.

"It's true my eyes aren't what they used to be," confessed the Potter, leaning back now on his arms. "But Clay, I hope you have learned by now, seeing isn't always done with your eyes. When it's done right –"

"It involves every atom of your being," said Clay, finishing the line.

"Sometimes eyes get in the way of seeing," said the Potter.

"Is that why I can move around you?"

The Potter shook his head. "Eyes have nothing to do with whether you can move or not."

"I moved around Dawne," said Clay, thinking about it.

"You can do anything, even if people believe that you can't."

"You mean, even if they can't see it?" asked Clay.

"Many things are missed when you only believe what you see." The Potter lifted his chin to the sky. "Beautiful, isn't it?"

Clay blinked in surprise. Sure enough, the sky was alive with ribbons of color. *Where had the day gone?* he wondered.

"To me, sunsets are far more than the diffusion of light particles through the atmosphere." The Potter's face was aglow in the fire-lit sky. "In all my years, I've yet to find a glaze to match it."

"Sunsets are pretty," said Clay, a twinge in his voice. To him, all a sunset did was remind him of how plain he looked.

"Nature is tough to top," said the Potter, as if to her.

She didn't respond (though the sky turned to blush).

"You know what is even more beautiful than a sunset?"

"Sunrises?" Clay guessed.

"No," laughed the Potter, "though sunrises can be breathtaking."

"What then?" Clay asked, gazing at the distance.

"Clay," he said.

"Yes?" he asked.

"Clay," repeated the Potter.

"Clay what?"

Suddenly, almost violently, the Potter took Clay by the shoulders. "Clay is a beautiful thing," he said.

Clay began to shake. He fought to look away, but the Potter's hands were powerful. Sunlight reflected off his storm cloud eyes like embers of fire, like light breaking through the clouds. The sight pierced the heart Clay did not have. It was painful. Clay trembled before it. He could not look away. "Clay," he said. "Clay," he whispered. "When will you see how wonderful it is to be Clay?"

Apple Trees

TWILIGHT VANISHED BEHIND the curtain of the world. Even with it being Indian Summer, it would be cold now that Twilight's light was gone. However, between Clay and the Potter things had become lighter. Understanding was peeking through like the stars peeking out from their spots in the sky, like the lights peeking out of cottage windows.

The Potter winced as he got to his feet: "Come, Clay. Movement will do us both good."

Clay stretched his legs.

"May I tell you a story?" the Potter asked as the two fell in step.

"Sure," said Clay.

"Thanks," he said, his arm coming around Clay's shoulder while his free hand painted the air. "Once upon a time there were two trees."

"What kind of trees?" asked Clay.

"Great question. Let's say they were apple trees."

"Did they grow in an orchard?"

"No," said the Potter. "They grew in different places: one, in the center of a town; the other, in a mountain valley."

"What variety were they?"

"McIntosh. No. Golden Delicious. I'm getting off subject. Anyway, both were wonderful trees; each produced big, juicy apples, right on time every fall."

"There's no apple tree in the center of town," said Clay.

"You're right. I should have been clearer. I was talking about another town."

"Where?" asked Clay.

"In my imagination."

"Oh," he said. Clay understood imagination. "Go on."

"Thank you," said the Potter, who was smiling though Clay couldn't see it. "Now, the tree in the center of town was famous. Folks came from miles to pick its fruit. Children climbed its branches. Young men proposed to young women in its shade. And every year, on the fall equinox, the townspeople threw it a party. They called it the Apple Festival. And underneath the tree, there was music, dancing, cider and hayrides. It was a fantastic celebration. They decorated the tree with ribbons and bows."

"Apple trees don't grow big enough to have dancing and hayrides under their branches."

"Perhaps I chose the wrong kind of tree," frowned the Potter.

"People would sprain their ankles on fallen apples and slip on the rotten ones," continued Clay, "and when it comes to cider, Golden Delicious do not make –"

"Those are very good points," laughed the Potter. "Let's say they danced in a lawn next to the tree, and the cider was imported."

"How about the cider came from the other tree?" suggested Clay.

"No," said the Potter. "The cider was imported from New Jersey, where there are no mountains. The other tree lived in a mountain valley."

"So what did the other tree do?" asked Clay.

"Well, it was a tree. It grew grand and wild, its fruit even juicier than the tree in town. As for its location – breathtaking, absolutely breathtaking – nestled between mountains, a happy stream beside it, wild-flowers and honeybees all around."

"Was it famous, too?" asked Clay.

"No one knew it existed," said the Potter, "except birds. Squirrels. A family of deer. But no people. There was no getting to it, not without difficulty."

"So it just sat there and did nothing?"

"Oh, it did something," said the Potter. "It grew."

"That's not much."

"It bore fruit."

"For no one."

"You see where my story is heading," said the Potter.

"You're saying that I'm like the tree in the mountain valley."

The Potter did not say.

Clay continued in the absence of words: "While other clays are meant to be made and have purpose and be celebrated, I am meant to be plain old clay."

"There is nothing wrong about growing where you are planted," said the Potter.

"I guess not," said Clay quietly. "It's just not very meaningful."

Stars twinkled from their spots in the universe.

"Tell me, Clay, which tree do you think was more valuable?"

"The tree in the town," murmured Clay.

"Yes," he said, "to the people in the town. But how about to Nature? Which tree was more valuable to her?"

"I don't know," said Clay. "I guess they were the same."

The Potter turned toward the heavens. His stormy eyes met the night. "Life is what really matters, not who eats the fruit."

"It matters to me," whispered Clay.

The Potter's hand left Clay's shoulder as he took a few steps toward the river. "What if I told you that one day a boy lost his way when exploring in the mountains? That evening, when he did not return, the townspeople searched for him. But found nothing. Not a sign. Days went by. His family feared the worst. No one could survive without nourishment and shelter. And they were right; no one could, not in those mountains. But what they didn't know was that the boy had stumbled into that quiet mountain valley. He had crawled to that marvelous, unknown tree. He had eaten its wonderful fruit. He had slept under its branches. They didn't know, that is, until the day a hiker stumbled up the hidden valley. And approaching the tree, would you believe the hiker's astonishment at seeing a boy safe and sound. Sick of apples, mind you, but no worse for wear."

"Is that really what happened?" asked Clay.

"It's my story," said the Potter. "I can tell it any way I want."

Clay's eyes searched the darkness as if to read it. He was trembling. He didn't know why. "What's mine?" he whispered.

The Potter's face was shrouded in shadows. It shifted from light to dark as the leaves danced in the night breeze. There happened to be a tree nearby.

"What do you want, my friend?" asked the Potter.

Clay opened the slice of his mouth but not a thing came out.

The Potter's question had caught him off guard. *What do you want?* It took a moment for the words to register. But now the full meaning came to him, and he was undone by it, overwhelmed by the sense that his entire existence had been a leading up to this moment – the creek bed, the orchard, the boy, the made things, the Crows, the anger, the confusion, the longings, the lostness, the waiting and waiting…the Potter and his patience and love – it all led to this. *What do you want, my friend?*

And quietly, Clay answered, the words coming out before he was certain that a choice had been made – as if the voice was someone else's, not his – and yet, it was his voice, of that he was certain. He said it. He heard it. He believed it with every mineral and molecule of his being: "I want to be Clay."

A Golden Age

WHAT HAPPENED NEXT was something not unlike a golden age. Looking back on it, that's what it was, a subtle shift that had transformed everything.

You see, now that Clay had let go of the expectation that the Potter was going to do something *to* him, he was able to grasp the wonder that the Potter was doing something *with* him. It created this new and strange satisfaction simply in being shaped each morning, this deep wonderment in being Clay.

He was whistling again.

Nothing else really changed. Clay worked, played and kept the Potter company the same as before. And yet, it was like everything that was the same was brand new.

The difference was: before, when the Potter asked, "Could you hold this for me?" Clay used to hear, "Carry my burdens." And so Clay did. He carried them, all the while feeling used (abused even), at the same time hoping that his effort might be rewarded, which only led to disappointment when nothing materialized. But now when the Potter asked, "Could you hold this for me?" Clay heard something different. He understood what the Potter meant. Because when the Potter said, "Could you hold this for me?" what he was really saying was, "Clay, I believe in you." Hearing that, Clay realized he didn't need a reward. In a sense, the action became one. So for instance, when the Potter lifted up a teapot and said: "What do you think of this handle?" Clay used to get jealous. He'd think that the Potter was saying, "Look how much better this clay is than you." But now, with this new perspective, Clay could see, even appreciate the object for what it was. He understood the words beneath the question. "What do you think of this handle?" meant, "Clay, your opinion matters to me." And now, Clay could offer one. He was no longer jealous. In fact, he wanted that teapot to have the best handle she could have. In other words, Clay's eyes were the same, but his *seeing* had changed. His ears were the same, but his *hearing* was different. His ordinary existence, which used to not be enough, suddenly became all he ever wanted. He was clay. Clay was *Clay*. And he wouldn't change a thing.

Life was golden.

And it remained that way –

– until the knock came.

Knock Knock

"IS ANYONE THERE?" asked a voice through the door.

"One moment," answered the Potter, mazing from the wedging table to the door.

Clay, who was sitting at the table beside a cube of kaolin, watched the door to see who was behind it. When he did, he almost fell to the floor.

It was Ned. The boy was three inches taller and had a dozen new freckles on his nose, but there was no mistaking him.

"Are you the Potter?" he asked, his voice a little grainy like it needed a motor to get it going.

"Why don't we find ourselves a seat," said the Potter, leading his guest to the wheel. He cleared the bench enough for two. "Would you like some tea?" he asked, motioning to the pot.

"No thanks."

"Mind if I do?" asked the Potter, pouring. He lifted the steaming cup to his lips, took a noisy sip then placed the cup in his lap: "So young man, how can I help you?"

"I," said Ned, before hesitating.

"Well, it can't be tea. I already tried that."

Ned shifted uncomfortably on the bench and leaned furtively before whispering: "I like clay."

"Me, too," said the Potter like he, too, was confiding a great secret.

Clay could almost see the tension lifting off the boy's shoulders. He cleared his throat: "Two summers ago, I played with some." His voice lowered again. "It was real."

"Of course it was," said the Potter.

"No. I mean, alive. It was almost alive," Ned said.

The Potter nodded.

Ned's eyes fell to his empty lap. "I didn't treat it very well. This summer, when I went back, it wasn't the same. There was only clay."

"There's no such thing as only clay," said the Potter. "The wonderful thing about Clay is that it can become anything."

"Maybe for you," Ned shrugged. "You're the Potter."

"Yes I am," said the Potter. "Would you like to see how it's done?"

Ned's countenance brightened.

The Potter continued, "It just so happens we were about to work with some on the wheel." Getting up, he shuffled to the wedging table and picked up the cube of kaolin next to Clay.

"That's Ned!" whispered Clay, "the boy I told you about."

"So it is," said the Potter. "Care to join us?" There was a twinkle of light peeking through his cataracts.

"I don't think I can move around him anymore," whispered Clay.

"Of course you can," said the Potter. "Follow me."

Reluctantly, Clay hopped to the floor.

Ned saw the movement out of the corner of his eye, but he figured it must have been a trick of the shadows. "Who were you talking to?" he asked.

"Clay," answered the Potter.

Had Clay any hair on his neck it would have prickled like a cat's back.

"Oh," said Ned, wondering if the man had lost his marbles. At the same time, crazy as it sounded, part of Ned wanted to believe.

"Take a look here," said the Potter, throwing the ball of clay on the wheel.

Clay crept to where the boy couldn't see him. Although soon it didn't matter because once the wheel spun to life, Ned was riveted.

Pat, pat, the Potter patted, the same way he patted Clayre last fall. The Potter dipped his hands in water, then hovered over the mound like a mother bird over her nest.

"First we must center," he said, guiding the clay into a cone.

Ned watched spellbound.

"Cone up," the Potter said.

"It looks like a trumpet," remarked Ned.

"Now that you mention it, he does resemble a trumpet," said the Potter, laughing. Wetting his hands once again, he said, "Down to center."

Amazed, Ned watched the clay obeyed the Potter's slightest touch.

"Hole in. Draw out the sides. Compress the bottom. Pull," the Potter said while he guided the kaolin clay into a cylinder.

"Are you doing that, or is it the clay?" asked Ned.

"Clay is the only one that changes," said the Potter.

"But are you the one who changes it?"

The Potter's lips curled into a smile. Without a word, he placed his hands on either side of the cylinder and widened it into a bowl.

"Ah!" cried Ned. "How did you do that?"

"Would you like to try?" asked the Potter.

"I don't think so," said Ned, even though it was obvious he wanted to try very much.

The Potter didn't press the matter. Using a string, he separated the bowl from the clay still on the wheel and placed it on a plank next to him. Then, toweling the excess clay off his finger, he returned to the wheel.

"People say you're magic," said Ned.

"Do they?" said the Potter, incapable of suppressing a grin.

Ned nodded. "They say you talk to clay like it's a friend."

"Of course," said the Potter, "Clay's good company."

"People say you're crazy."

"I don't care what people say," the Potter said plainly.

"They say that, too," said Ned, chuckling.

The Potter continued to work at the wheel. Next to him, the wheels in Ned's head were working, too. It grew quiet between them. Until finally, with a set of bowls complete, the Potter dried his muddy hands down the thighs of his pant legs and gave the boy a wink. "Yes, Ned," he said with a grin warm and fatherly, "you may come back tomorrow."

The next day, Ned came as soon as school let out. In fact, Ned came most days that fall. As you might expect, the Potter was a patient teacher, so patient it stirred Ned's *im*patience at times, though the two got along fairly well. Ned was a good student, meaning he listened, didn't assume, and was willing to try. He even cleaned up afterward.

Clay kept his distance during the lessons. He'd tiptoe behind a sack of ash or spy between two containers of glaze; though inevitably, he'd knock over a jar or fail to realize that his hindquarters were exposed.

Ned never brought up the fact that a boy-shaped mound of clay seemed to be following him around the studio. He no longer believed it was possible that clay could move by itself.

No one in their right mind believed that. There were moments when he wondered, but they always came out of context, and he found them awkward to talk about – even with the Potter, who would have understood. Thinking back on it, the Potter probably knew what was happening even without the talking about it.

Clay, too, was finding it hard to believe. How Ned had suddenly reentered his life – it was pretty unexpected, and incredible when he thought about it. The pain of their last encounter was gone. And Ned had changed. That much was clear. He wouldn't have come otherwise. But it was deeper than that. Clay saw it in the boy's face the afternoon he retrieved his first piece of pottery out of the kiln. It was a small cylinder, thick and uneven with a slant to one side. But to Ned it was beautiful. Who cared if the glazes had congealed into a greenish beet color? Ned loved it. And Clay felt a pang of jealousy toward it – especially the day Ned carried it home.

The truth was Clay felt a pang every time Ned left the Potter's house. In the evening, as the boy said goodbye and disappeared into dusk, Clay longed to go with him. Not that he didn't also want to stay. There was gold-enness to his relationship with the Potter. But Ned was young and pliable; he was still forming into what he would one day become. And it mattered very much to Clay how Ned turned out.

Thinking back on it, the Potter probably knew this as well.

The Gift

IT WAS NEARING Christmas and the Potter was busy filling orders, Ned was busy making presents, and Clay would stretch into a snake in order to keep an eye on both of them. As you can imagine, the Potter's work was exquisite. However, Clay often found himself drawn to the not-so-exquisite things Ned was making.

There was the mixing bowl for Mother, the one he hoped would fit inside the nesting bowls Father had given her last year. Ned made a mug for him. It was sturdy and large since Father was always getting up for refills. He was pretty sure he'd like it. Betsy, on the other hand, was getting a butterfly. It was partly a joke because last year Ned had said that he hoped she'd been given one so that his frog figurine could have something to eat, but it was also partly because butterflies were beautiful, and Betsy (who was going by Elizabeth now) was becoming that way herself.

Of course, the most meaningful thing about the gifts was that Ned made them, a fact that went double for the teacup he made for the Potter. Through it, Ned hoped to show his mentor two things: first, how much he learned; and second, how grateful he was for being taught. It was why he kept the cup secret, going so far as to fire it underneath a bowl; he wanted to make sure that everything was just right before the Potter laid his hands on it. Of all Ned's gifts, he spent the most time and effort on the Potter's teacup. And you could tell by the way it turned out. Even so, Ned's hands were shaking the afternoon he handed the gift to him. Ned was well aware that the Potter, with a twirl of the wheel, could whip one up twice as good. It was why his voice cracked when he said, "I made this for you."

Clay looked on from behind a barrel.

The Potter took the cup in his hands. He felt the rim with the soft part of his index finger. He slid his palm along the foot (the bottom). He turned it for balance. Then, nodding with approval, he asked, "Mind if I try her?"

Ned didn't mind at all.

"I have something for you as well," he said, sipping loudly once the tea had been poured.

"What?" asked Ned eagerly.

"It could be anything," answered the Potter, his eyes closing in wistful crescents.

"So it's a surprise," said Ned, a little disappointed. (As true as it is that everyone enjoys surprises, no one really does before they happen.)

The Potter's eyes were misty and incomprehensible, but warm. "Can you come tomorrow for it?" he asked. "I'll wrap it along with the rest of your gifts."

Ned thanked him and promised to return.

Clay watched the boy run out the door.

The Potter put his hand on Clay's shoulder.

That evening, the Potter and Clay took a long walk by the river with no purpose whatsoever although looking back, it may have been the most meaningful of all the walks they shared. Many things passed between them; most were personal, too personal for me to write them here. Suffice it to say that the interaction was tender and sweet. Tears gathered in the storm clouds of the Potter's eyes – a salty mixture of joy and sorrow – and Clay felt the same though he possessed no tears to show it.

And at some point during the evening, in one of their exchanges or perhaps in one of the pauses, something stirred inside of Clay. It was like a candle flickering to life in the place his heart would have been, like the missing part was not missing anymore. Because the Potter once again showed Clay what the Potter had been showing him all along: Clay had purpose, a wonderful one. He always did and always would. And finally, Clay was able to embrace it because finally Clay understood. The Potter had made him after all. The Potter had made him whole.

It was like he was wiping tears away.

Christmas Eve

THE FOLLOWING DAY, Ned returned to the Potter's house while his family huddled in the horse cart. They were heading to the orchard for the holiday, and Ned had insisted they make the stop. The Potter was expecting him, he explained.

It was true. Early that morning, the Potter had wrapped each one of Ned's presents and packed them in a wooden box full of straw. Ned's gift was wrapped in cheesecloth and placed in a burlap sack with the instruction that it might be best for it to be opened in private. "Your mother might not approve," the Potter said with a wink. Ned smiled. They embraced.

"Speaking of Mother, she made this for you," Ned said, handing him a Mason jar of apple butter. "She said it was one of her best batches ever."

"I'm glad to hear it," said the Potter, beaming with delight. "Now I have something to bring to the Christmas feast." He cradled the gift in his arm and walked Ned and Clay to the door. "Bye, friends."

"Bye," said Ned, taking his seat, the package next to him.

Through a tiny tear, Clay watched the Potter fade in the shadow of the doorframe. He watched until the horse cart bumped away.

Ned held him close. The frozen road was bumpy. The air was brittle. Steam flared from the horse's nostrils. Ice covered the shallows along Mule Lick Creek. The cold came through the boards beneath their britches. And by the time the Farmers reached the orchard, the thrill of spending the holiday in the hill country had diminished to shivers and runny noses.

Clay was cold, too, though he didn't need to worry about becoming hard. The Potter had wrapped him as snug as a caterpillar in a chrysalis.

Ned carried his gift upstairs. Kicking the door shut, he dropped the burlap sack on the quilt. He pulled back the cheesecloth, enough to reveal Clay's head. "I knew it," he whispered, smiling. "I was hoping." Clay looked at the boy through two wide poked eyes: "You won't believe this," he whispered, "but I used to play with clay like you. I always wanted him to visit my room. We got close once, but we didn't make it. And now you're here."

Clay's slice of a mouth curled upwards, but Ned failed to see it.

"I called him Clay. Is it all right if I call you that?" Ned could hardly believe he was talking to a lump of clay, though he could have sworn he heard a faint, familiar whistle coming from it.

"Ned," called Elizabeth from downstairs, "Father's making us cut down a Christmas tree. Don't think you're getting out of it."

"Be right there," shouted Ned. He carried Clay to a table by the window. "See you later, Clay. Maybe after, we can form part of you into a friend for my frog figurine."

Ned bounded to the door.

When the downstairs grew quiet, Clay slipped from his sack. Venturing out the door, he descended to the main room. Circled the family table. Touched the stone hearth. From the window, he followed the Farmers until they disappeared into a grove of evergreens.

Later, from the top of the stairwell, he watched the family dress the chosen tree with tinsel, balls and strings of popped corn. Buttery chicken stew steamed toward him. Biscuits and apple butter, too. The smell was so glorious he could almost taste it. And judging by how fast supper was eaten, it must have tasted as good as the aroma. All throughout, Clay leaned through the rails, listening to dinner conversation. He remained there as afterward Ned suggested they play some music like the old times (which they all thought was funny because Ned was not very old). They agreed; and once the dishes were washed and put away, Father tuned his banjo, Mother wiped the dust off the piano keys, and the four sang the songs they all knew by heart.

Outside, the world played a different tune. That afternoon, an icy wind had rolled in from the west. It rattled the windows like a prisoner behind bars. It seeped through the walls like a dam about to break. The floorboards groaned like a ghost story.

On nights like this, Clay would have frozen stiff in his deposit. It brought a smile to his face as he flexed his knees and elbows because tonight wasn't ordinary. He wasn't in his deposit. He was here, inside, with Ned and his family. It was a wondrous reality, made all the better by the extraordinariness of it.

Downstairs, the Farmers sang until all four of them were reduced to yawns and eye rubbings. Father threw a few extra logs on the fire and plucked quietly on the strings of his banjo when Mother told the children it was time to go to bed. *Time for me, too,* Clay thought to himself as he slipped back to Ned's room and pulled the burlap over his head. Seconds later, Father entered holding a half-asleep Ned against his chest. He tucked the boy in without taking off his clothes. He kissed him on the forehead. And Ned said, "Good night." He said it twice.

Clay wondered if the second words had been for him. He hoped so. He'd have to wait until morning to find out, but at least tonight, the hope warmed him against the icy air creeping through his fabric.

The ruthless wind shook the house once again.

"John, would you take an extra quilt to the children?" he heard Mother ask.

Stairs creaked. The door handle moved. The door closed again.

Ned's breathing was heavy.

The wind shrieked like wheels on a freight train.

Clay hugged his arms tight around his body. Still, he shivered in the burlap. Like the Potter's shoes, it was holey. Through one, he could see out the window. The stars were out. They twinkled from their spots in the universe without a care. Wind, storms, the difficulties of this world never bothered them. They sparkled just the same. For a flexible object like Clay, their consistency was something to admire.

He closed the hole as best he could, surprised that such a small gap could let in so much cold air. He was trying not to think about it when he became distracted by noises: the slam of the outhouse door, the sad creak of shutters, the whipping of a rope gone loose. The wind. It was so loud it was almost all he could hear. It was like the wind could consume noise. Devour it. He heard crying. Funny how the wind could mimic sounds like that – crying, whistling, howling, screaming – the wind could do it all. This wind sounded just like voices.

The house quaked.

Screaming. Shouting. Crying.

Clay shot up.

That wasn't wind.

He poked his head out of his sack. Odd. There was light underneath the door. It wasn't moonlight or starlight or lamplight; it was pulsing orange…like…fire!

Clay threw off his covers. He didn't fiddle with the latch. He shouldered the door open and faced the horror.

The first floor was engulfed in flames. Smoke billowed up the stairwell.

It was impossible to see. But he heard voices. They were screaming. Crying.

A timber crashed to the floor.

Clay ran back into the room.

He shook Ned.

The boy coughed.

He helped him to his feet.

The floor was hot.

There was no time for shoes.

There was no time –

– Mother, Father and Elizabeth huddled in the frozen grass.

They were safe.

They were crying.

Mother crumbled to the earth. Elizabeth put her arms around her. Father blinked blankly then put his arms around the both of them.

His back was like a shield. Firelight beat against it.

Shadows danced like demons.

Helplessly, Father turned toward the house. Fire reflected coldly in his eyes.

The cries of his wife and daughter drowned in the howling wind.

There was nothing he could have done. There was nothing now to do.

Wicked orange flame filled the doorframe.

No one, nothing, emerged.

The wind whipped the door shut.

Fire spewed from the windows.

Inside, there were splintering crashes.

Shattering glass.

Devastating energy.

Eerie silence.

The absence of life.

Ned was gone.

The morning was cold.

Christmas Morning

CRUEL SMOKE DRIFTED aimlessly to a cloudless sky. The fire had burned itself out for the most part. Besides a few smoldering crackles, the silence was palpable.

Mother's eyes were red with sleeplessness and tears. Father's were blank with loss. They had spent the night with the Thrift family who owned the farm upstream. James and Eliza were good people. Eliza stayed awake with Mother most the night until she finally convinced Mother to lie down and rest awhile. James said he would go with Father to the house in the morning. In the end, they all went. They were compelled even if it was with reluctance.

The house was a black shell. Glass was on the ground below the windows. A shutter lay unblemished in the grass. The door was gone except for the iron handle. It rested beneath the doorframe like a disregarded toy.

Father kicked the burnt banister that led to the front porch. It broke in two.

By accident Elizabeth said the forbidden word. The day before it had just been the name she called her brother. Now, having said it, she realized she would never say it again without crying. Tears streaked down her cheeks. She hid her face in Mother's dress. Mother put her hand on her head.

News of the disaster had spread, and folks were arriving in clusters – friends and neighbors ready to pitch in – but they all pretty much stood there and did nothing. Because what do you do when a family has lost a son?

Finally, the men set to work, filling buckets in the creek and carrying them in a kind of procession. One after the other they doused the house. Sick smoke steamed to the sky. The smell was rotten.

It was obvious the house was cool enough to enter though no one seemed to be in a hurry to go inside. It was like they were waiting for John Farmer, which they were.

In the end, James Thrift went with him. He was a skinny fellow with yellow teeth and wisps of hair that served no purpose whatsoever.

The two men stepped inside. Truly, it was a miracle the house was standing at all. It was only a matter of time before it wasn't. The men trod lightly in that awareness. Beneath their feet, the floorboards groaned forebodingly. The walls were charred. Black holes poked through the ceiling. The dining room table lay legless on the floor. There was a hole through the middle. A destroyed painting clung to its hook. Banjo strings curled like grotesque fingernails. The stone hearth gaped like a mouth locked in a nightmare scream. Its coals had been the culprit. A wind gust had come down the chimney and sprayed embers across the floor.

"What's that?" James Thrift asked. Glass broke underneath his heel.

"Where you looking?" asked John Farmer, bending over his banjo.

"The nook beneath the stairs. It looks like, well, it's hard to describe, but I'd say it's a bowl."

"Bowl?"

"Over there," said James Thrift, "upside-down."

"What in the world?" said John Farmer, crossing the room.

"Biggest bowl I've ever seen."

"That's not a bowl," said John Farmer. "I believe that's...Clay!"

"Clay?" asked James Thrift.

"He must have been made by the fire. But how?"

James Thrift scratched his head. "You hear that?"

"*Ssshhh.* I hear it, too."

"It's coming from inside, I think."

The two men placed their ears to the strange object on the floor.

"It sounds like knocking," said James Thrift.

John knocked against Clay's rough, biscuit-fired surface.

A knock came back.

"Good Lord, somebody's inside!"

"Ned!" cried his Father.

James Thrift grunted. "The bowl won't budge. It's cemented to the floorboards."

"There's a hammer in my toolbox. In the shed," said John Farmer frantically.

James Thrift hurried out.

Father caressed Clay's grainy surface. "Don't worry, Son. We'll get you out of there."

Ned said something that Father was unable to understand.

James Thrift returned. He handed the hammer to his neighbor.

The hammer came down.

Clay broke to pieces.

Father and son embraced amidst the shards.

Epilogue

Afterward by the Fire

GRANDPA GREW SILENT.

Between us, the coals in the fireplace beat like a heart. A solitary lamp glowed by the window. Its light glanced off his silver hair that always stayed just so.

"So what happened?" I asked.

Orange embers reflected in his cloudy eyes. It was dark, but I could tell he was looking at me. "Many things," he said.

"What do you mean?" I asked.

"Well, I completed my studies. Met a lady. We married. Had three daughters. They had children. We had grandchildren. You were our first, Ned."

Our eyes met. Grandpa and his namesake.

"You would not have happened if Clay had not been made."

A chill passed through me.

"I'm alive because of him. The same is true for you, Grandson. There is freedom in that. And responsibility."

"What happened to Clay?" I asked.

Tears gathered in Grandpa's eyes. Tears were in mine as well.

"He broke to pieces," he said, a hollow despair in his voice.

"Don't tell me you took him to the dump!"

Grandpa didn't say.

"Where?" I asked. I needed to know.

But Grandpa shook his head. Closing his eyes, he exhaled. And in the silence I understood. Clay was dead. It happened years ago. The night of the fire.

Though at the moment, his death was near. I could feel it in the silence – see it in the tears that streamed down the creases of Grandpa's cheeks. He saw it against the walls of his eyelids.

He didn't say another word.

Neither did I.

But for the fireplace's *hiss* of heat, it was quiet. It was quiet for a long time.

The coals lost their color. It was odd, but now that the fire was gone, I could see better. The realization sidetracked me for a moment, only a moment, for there was something about Grandpa's story that bothered me.

But it was too late to ask.

He was asleep. I could hear it in Grandpa's breathing.

I extinguished the lamp by the window. On the other side of the pane, stars sparkled from their spots in the universe. I thought about Clay, staring from his spot by the creek, wondering if there was more to life than just being what he was.

I wondered if anything in Grandpa's story was true. Surely, Clay was not. Who ever heard of a walking, talking, thinking, feeling piece of dirt? Clay was a metaphor, a character Grandpa made up for a young, pliable, restless boy – *like me.*

"I am Clay," I whispered, my words clouding the windowpane, my heart stirring inside of me. This was Grandpa's way of telling me to be patient with the process – that as wonderful as it is to become something, the greatest thing to become is oneself. I turned toward him. I watched him breathe, the whole of my being swelling with love and gratitude for the love Grandpa had for me.

Still, I felt disappointment. Grandpa's story had been just that – a story. Clay wasn't real. What happened really hadn't. Somehow, that truth made the meaning less so.

The silvery strands of Grandpa's hair rose and fell. They crested the back of the chair. I didn't want to disturb him, but I noticed there was a blanket folded under his arm. I walked over and took hold of it. His arm moved. His hand opened. Something fell to the floor. I bent down. The ground was cast in shadow, but I found what had fallen. I felt it.

"Could it be?" I whispered.

The shard in my hand was rough, warm, and moist from being held so long. The edges were uneven and dull. I raised it against the night. "Clay?" I whispered.

Grandpa's chin rested in the cradle of his collar. His breathing was quiet waves along a shoreline.

When from somewhere very close, very softly, I heard…*whistling.*

THE END

Author's Note

WHEN I ARRIVED freshman year at college, I was introduced to this new thing. Along with a dorm room and a class schedule, each first year student was given an electronic identification code. It was incredible what you could do with it. For instance, you could type a message on your computer, and, by using electronic identification codes, you could send that message to another person's computer by addressing it to their electronic identification code. They called it "electronic mail" or "e-mail" for short. All without stamps or floppy disks. Like I said, incredible.

My grandfather was an engineer and, therefore, always ahead of the curve when it came to technology. I remember playing Invaders on his Texas Instruments TI-99 back in 1980. They sure don't make them like that anymore. He and his colleagues had been e-mailing for years. And now that he finally had a family member with an e-mail address, he had someone with whom to electronically share his non-work related thoughts. Thus began our correspondence.

One afternoon, I was checking my inbox when up popped a message from my Grandpa's prodigy.net account. I opened it and began reading.

I could tell right away it was different from the other messages he sent me. For one, it was long. Grandpa's notes were usually short and included questions like: how are your classes? This one went on for two pages with no paragraph breaks.

It was a story about how every weekend he used to travel back and forth from the University of Delaware to Pittsburgh in order to spend time with the woman who eventually became my grandmother. There were only two lane roads back then and not very good ones. And Grandpa would stay in Pittsburgh with Lena until the last possible moment on Sunday before hopping in the car and driving through the night to make it just in time for his 8:30 class Monday morning. I chuckled when I read that because Grandpa in later years became notorious for nodding off at the wheel. Perhaps it was from the sleep deprivation he suffered from these all night drives.

Well one night, he was driving back to Delaware through extremely dense fog. It was late, going on two in the morning, when on the side of the road, Grandpa noticed a person frantically waving his arms. Grandpa hit the brakes and got out of the car to discover something strange. *No one was there.* He called out. No one answered. Confused, he got out and searched the darkness. No sign of an accident. No sign of anything. He walked to the front of his car. It was then he heard it.

Water. Lots of it. Ten feet from his front bumper, invisible in the fog, a bridge was out. He never would have been able to stop in time.

The person waving his arms on the side of the road, the one who had vanished in thin air, had saved Grandpa's life!

The e-mail continued. Grandpa confessed that to that point in his life he had never given faith much of a thought. He was a man of science and believed in rational explanations for things. But in the last fifty some-odd years, the only explanation he had been able to come up with for the events of that night was divine intervention. God had sent an angel.

Grandpa went on to share about how he spent much of his life wondering why it happened, why he had been spared. He wrote about the freedom and responsibility that comes from questions like that. Then, he wrote words that give me chills to this day: He said that when I was born, that when he held me for the first time, the memory of that night by the washed out bridge came to his mind. He hadn't thought about it for years. But looking at me it was like God was telling him: "This is the reason you were saved."

Grandpa wrote some other things, most were personal, too personal for me to write them here. Suffice to say, his words were tender and sweet.

We never discussed his e-mail.

On January 23, 2009 I had a dream. Perhaps you dream, too. This one was unlike any I had ever had. I was Clay. I could twist, jump, stretch, roll, walk, talk and whistle, just like you and me. But something was missing. It's hard to describe, but inside of me there was this deep longing – this restless desire to be more than what I was.

The story you have just read is my dream. That's right. I dreamed the whole thing: the Bricks, China, Prayer for a Daughter, the Potter, the running away, the putting back together, the words he shared by the river about how wonderful it is to be Clay, words that still put tears in my eyes. Even the fire. The becoming made in the end. I dreamed it all.

Two weeks later, my son David was born. Holding him for the first time, I couldn't escape the memory of that dream. It was like God was telling me: "This is the reason." David and his sister Anna Rose: I was made for them.

My purpose is not my own.

Since then, I've been coming to grips with this dream, leaning tentatively into the freedom that comes with knowing there is no better thing to become than oneself. The responsibility comes in what you do with the freedom – the who and the what you lay down your life for.

That's why I believe this is a true story. Not that there was ever a creek called Mule Lick or a brownstone deposit along its banks. But that what happened to Clay has happened to me. It's my story. And perhaps you have found your story here, too.

Ned

Acknowledgments

FIRST OF ALL, thank you. By reading *Clay*, you have fulfilled its purpose. I only hope that what you have read in these pages encourages you in the quest for yours. It has for me. It may surprise you to know that I continue to learn things from *Clay*. I have a strong feeling that this story will accompany me the rest of my life. And I couldn't be more thankful.

It's for this reason I am compelled to thank the following people because without their help and encouragement, *Clay* would never have become made.

Mom and Pops, what we believe defines us. And your belief has made me into a writer. Thank you.

Karen Teears, thank you for championing this book even when victory slipped through our fingers.

Fil Anderson, you love me despite what you know. And there is no higher thing than to be known and loved.

Powen Liu, you are a far better instructor than what my pottery suggests. Thank you for your patience. This book could not have been written without you.

Teresa Tsipis, Caitlin Forlan, Tom Shaver, and the Summit School Class of 2017, thank you for being early readers. Your illustrations and feedback were invaluable.

Joan Mitchell, thank you for taking your mastery of English and applying it to this humble text.

Kim and Crick Watkins, thank you for your expertise and the lending of your name. Glad my evil plan to keep you as neighbors has worked thus far.

Robert Milam, folks are going to buy this book just because of your cover art. Thank you my friend. And thank you, Trevor Mork, for the photo.

Beth Williams, I want the world to read this book just so they can see your amazing illustrations. You and Cooper will always be lifers to Lia and me.

To the men who have dubbed themselves "Ned Ink," thank you. Lesser (and perhaps smarter) men would have given up on me long ago. Mike Edens, Clyde Godwin and Scott Steele, you are friends to the end. I wouldn't wish all the failure, disappointment, and rejection I have experienced on anyone, but I do wish everyone could experience what it's like to have friends go with you through it all.

To Young Life, no other organization has shaped my understanding of God or myself as much as you. I could not be more grateful.

To Hope Church, you are the closest thing our family has found to the bar in Cheers.

Caroline Cox, few people – actually come to think of it, a lot of people – know how much I need help. Few are crazy enough to help me. Thank you for being one.

Anna Rose and David, I thought of you when I wrote, "it mattered very much to Clay how Ned turned out." It does. But it matters most to me that you know this: I love you right now. No matter what your future holds, I will love you. Anna Rose and David, you will always be wonderful to your mother and me.

Speaking of your mother . . . Lia, what can I say? How do I express the deepest parts of my soul? Only you know. I wonder if you'll ever know.

About the Author

NED ERICKSON LIVES in Winston-Salem, North Carolina with his family. A writer, speaker, musician, and amateur potter, he has served for many years with Young Life.

ALSO BY NED
*Falling Into Love: How an Average Guy
Got the Girl of his Dreams*

Please consider Ned for your next event, service, camp, assembly, meeting or retreat.

CONTACT INFORMATION
Ned Erickson
851 W. 5th Street
Winston-Salem, NC 27101
claythebook@gmail.com
nederickson.com
nederickson.blogspot.com

Made in the USA
Middletown, DE
28 July 2016